WILDE NIGHTS IN PARADISE

A WILDE SECURITY NOVEL

TONYA BURROWS

Previously released on Entangled's Brazen imprint — June 2013

Entangled Publishing, LLC
2614 South Timberline Road
Suite 109
Fort Collins, CO 80525
Visit our website at www.entangledpublishing.com.

Ignite is an imprint of Entangled Publishing, LLC.

Edited by Heather Howland
Cover design by Heather Howland
Cover art from iStock

Manufactured in the United States of America

First Edition June 2013

ignite

To Shauna.
My sister, my best friend.
Love ya!

Chapter One

Thirty-one days.

And counting.

Really. Fucking. Slowly.

Jude Wilde groaned and leaned back in his office chair. Maybe leaving the Marines hadn't been the best decision of his thirty years. Of course, nobody could ever accuse him of having good decision-making skills, so there was no sense in breaking that tradition now.

Still. Had it really been only a month since he got out? At least the Marines, with all of their political BS, had offered stimulation, distraction, entertainment.

But *this*?

He scanned the mostly empty office space of Wilde Security—industrial gray carpet, banged-up metal desks, walls that may have been white back in the days of Nixon—until his gaze found two of his older brothers, Camden and Vaughn.

"You know," he said, "this P.I. stuff is not as cool as it seems in the movies."

Ever competitive, the twins were busy arguing over another game of Battleship, and he got no response.

Sighing, Jude tilted his head back and spun his chair around and around until his stomach started to spin right along with the ceiling. He stopped. Straightened. Wobbled. Glowered at his brothers again. "Guys, seriously, I'm so freakin' bored. I'm gonna lose my mind here."

"Quick, hide the matches," Camden said and finally looked up. "And the scissors, paper clips, and anything else shiny or pointy."

"Can't have little brother hurting himself," Vaughn added with a shit-eating grin, then proceeded to sink Cam's sub.

Jude grabbed a sheet of paper from the blank pad on his desk, wadded it up. He sent it sailing toward the twins and had the great satisfaction of watching it nail Vaughn in the face before it bounced and smacked Cam on the side of the head.

Jude held up his arms. "Goaaal!"

The twins shared a glance, communicating in their freaky nonverbal way, and—oh, shit!—he had just enough time to leap out of his chair before they launched across the office.

Two against one, just like when they were kids. Even calling on every ounce of military training he possessed, Jude didn't stand a chance. Still, a friendly brawl with his brothers was a helluva lot better than stewing in his own boredom. A good wrestling match always livened things up, especially if he could turn the twins against each other. Then he'd sneak out of the fray, sit back, and watch the show.

Cam went in low, tackling him around the middle while

Vaughn went high. The combined force of four hundred pounds of muscle made for a jarring impact and wrenched the air from his lungs, but he still croaked out a laugh.

"Guys, you're getting soft—" An elbow plowed into his gut. "Umph."

All right. Time to weasel his way out before a blow landed farther south. He grabbed two handfuls of someone's T-shirt—ah, Camden's. Perfect—and yanked the fabric up. Blinded, Cam lost his balance and slammed fist-first into Vaughn, who growled and shoved his twin hard. The three of them went down in a cursing knot of flailing limbs. Cam shrugged out of the tangled shirt and grabbed Vaughn in a headlock. Jude took the opportunity to scramble out from under the dog pile, skull dragging across the carpet until a polished shoe blocked his path.

Shit.

Wincing, he gazed up from the glossy Italian leather, followed the crease of perfectly pleated trousers and the gray pinstripes of a silk tie to meet his second-oldest brother's glowering hazel eyes. "Reece. Hi."

At the sound of Reece's name, the twins jumped apart like repelled magnets. Cam was still shirtless and had earned himself a swollen lip. Vaughn would be sporting a black eye by the end of the afternoon. Both were breathing hard, and Jude had to bite the inside of his cheek to stifle a laugh. Those two were just too damn easy to rile up.

Reece's mouth turned down at the corners. A small frown, but enough to tell Jude just how pissed big bro was. Yet Reece effortlessly smoothed his expression into a pleasant smile and turned to the man standing beside him, who looked like a cover model for *GQ* with his streaky, salon-styled blond hair and straight, bleached teeth.

"Mr. Burke, these are our investigators, my brothers Camden, Vaughn, and Jude. They practice their hand-to-hand combat techniques daily and often test each other with surprise attacks. Unfortunately, that sometimes means a scuffle breaks out in the office."

"In the office?" Burke looked down his straight nose at Jude, a slight sneer pulling up the corner of his mouth. "That's highly irregular."

"And what makes us the best at handling *irregular* situations." Reece waved an arm toward the back of the building, where Greer, their oldest brother and founder of Wilde Security, held court. "If you'll follow me, Greer's office is this way. He's anxious to talk specifics with you and your client."

The office door shut behind them, and Jude said, "Ruh-roh."

"You are such a little shithead," Vaughn replied and touched his already-swollen eye.

"Yeah, but you two make such easy targets."

Cam parted his lips, no doubt to lash out with a retort, but the office door opened again, and Reece reappeared. Ruh-roh was right. Reece's gaze all but singed as he zeroed in on each of them in turn.

"Cam, put on a goddamn shirt," he snapped. "Vaughn, go ice your eye. And *you*." He pinned Jude with a finger, much the same as their father used to when they were kids. "You better fucking behave. Kenneth Burke represents a big client. We're talking a bigger payday than we've ever seen, and you are *not* going to screw us up." The *for once in your life* part went unspoken. It never had to be said. They all knew Jude was the family fuck up, and he'd made his peace with that.

"Greer wants you three in here for this," Reece continued. "So pull your act together and at least pretend you're
professionals."

Jude snapped into a salute. "Yes, sir."

Reece just shook his head and shoved back into the
office, grumbling something under his breath about little
brothers. Dude really needed to loosen up. It must be exhausting to stay wound so tight twenty-four/seven. Sometimes shit happened, and no amount of planning in the
world stopped it from happening, so why worry? That was
Jude's philosophy. Have fun when life was good. Bend over
and take it when shit got bad. And never, ever look back.
Bridges burned for a reason. He made sure of it because the
past hurt too damn much.

One of the twins socked him in the shoulder as they
passed.

"Good going," Vaughn said.

"Now he's gonna be in a pisser of a mood all day," Cam
added.

"When isn't he?" Jude wondered aloud as he fell into
step behind the twins. Reece's middle name was Stick-Up-
The-Ass, and his smiles were few and far between.

But if smiling was a rarity for Reece, it was a completely
foreign concept to the eldest Wilde brother.

Greer sat behind his disaster area of a desk, faint scowl
lines creasing his forehead, his eyes narrowed in displeasure.
Even though he'd been out of the military for almost a year,
he still wore his dark hair shaved to the scalp.

And he looked like Dad.

The similarity smacked Jude in the face, and he stopped

short just inside the door, struggling against an immediate urge to apologize for…well, everything.

Sorry I never listened, Dad. Sorry I caused you and Mom so much heartache.

Sorry I killed you.

No. He shook his head. Not Dad. Greer. It was Greer sitting there, watching him with those dark, dark eyes.

Jude turned away to shut the office door, needing that extra second to school his features back into an affable smile. His cheeks hurt, the muscles pulling, and he worked his jaw to loosen everything up until he could smile without wanting to scream.

Yup. Bridges burned for a reason.

With his usual smile firmly in place, he faced his brothers, who studied him with expressions ranging from worried—the twins—to disinterested—Reece—to completely unreadable—Greer. Burke, the new client, sat regally in a wood fold-up chair in front of Greer's desk and acted like they were all too far below him to rate much of his attention.

"Go over it again for my brothers," Greer told the man.

Burke's gaze shifted to the twins, who no doubt made an intimidating pair if you didn't know them. They both grinned like cats in sight of prey, and Burke sniffed disdainfully. "To be perfectly frank, this is a waste of time and money."

"Again," Greer commanded in his Army Ranger voice.

Burke pursed his lips. "Of course. I'm a lawyer, and the family I represent is facing a sensitive problem…"

Jude lounged against the wall and dipped a hand in his pocket, jiggling the ring he carried with him everywhere as he settled in for what was sure to be a mind-numbingly long story. If he had a dollar for every time a client came to Wilde

Security in the past month with a "sensitive" problem... Well, he sure the hell wouldn't be working here.

Aruba was nice this time of year. Or any time of year.

He'd be lounging on a white sand beach with a sissy frou-frou drink—because what else did you drink in beach fantasies?—and a beautiful woman cradled in his lap. A blonde. Yeah, but not an out-of-the-bottle blonde. Natural, with golden tones that matched the gold flecks in her light brown eyes. She'd be wearing a purple string bikini with ties at the hips, and as he offered her his drink, he'd reach down and pull the knots loose. She'd laugh and take off her square, black-framed glasses—

Wait. No. His Aruban fantasy woman did *not* have glasses. Or a purple string bikini. Or anything else that he associated with...*her*.

And yet he could picture it—and her—so clearly, he could almost smell the vanilla spice perfume she always used to wear.

"Goddammit!"

Everyone in the room turned toward him, and he cursed again, silently this time. Greer's eyes narrowed in warning. Reece made a low grumbling sound in his throat. The twins both struggled to maintain their professional faces.

"Sorry." He scrambled to find a plausible excuse for his outburst, but all he came up with was a pathetic, "Saw a big-ass spider. Hate those things."

Greer waved a dismissive hand. "Go on," he said to the client, who appeared even more contemptuous now than before.

Jude pushed away from the wall and made himself pay attention to the man. He couldn't screw this up or his brothers would murder him. So no more fantasies about Aruba or… *her*. He smiled at Burke, turning his internal charm-o-meter up from stun to devastate. "Yes, please, Mr. Burke, go on. I apologize for the interruption."

Burke opened the briefcase on his lap and produced a slim folder, handing it to Greer. "I'm sure this is not necessary, but my client insists we hire one of you to protect his daughter. I have the file right here."

Pushing aside a stack of papers to make room, Greer opened the folder. On top lay a dossier with a photograph of a woman clipped to it.

A blond woman.

With square, black-framed glasses.

She stared out from the photo, all cool confidence with her hair twisted up on top of her head and her eyes level on the camera, so different from the last time Jude had seen her. Eight years ago, her face had been splotchy and smeared with lines of mascara from the tears streaming down her cheeks. Her hair had been falling out of its clip. Her lips had quivered as she approached him at the bar. He'd fully expected her to slap him and had steeled himself against it, but the pain in her brown eyes as she dropped his engagement ring into his beer had been far more effective than a slap.

Those eyes had haunted him for years.

Jude moved closer to the desk to get a better look and experienced a dizzying sense of déjà vu. No fucking way. It couldn't be *her*. It couldn't be…

"What's her name?" Greer asked.

"Elizabeth Pruitt," Burke said at the same time Jude whispered, "Libby."

Burke's head snapped around so fast he must have given

himself whiplash. "Do you know her?"

Greer arched a brow, but Jude ignored them both and picked up her photo. The last eight years had been kind to her. Very kind. Even his Aruban fantasy version of her hadn't done her justice. He traced the elegant line of her cheek, remembered doing the same as they lay tangled together on the living room floor of her college apartment with the sun streaming through the open window...

"Jude!" Greer's sharp voice brought him back to the present, and he forced his gaze away from the photo. "You know her?"

"Used to." He set the photo back on the desk, but it took a lot more effort to let the damn thing go than it should have. "Not anymore."

At that moment, the door opened, and in walked a barge of man that Jude never thought he'd see again. Time had been kind to Colonel Elliot Pruitt, too. Save for the receding hairline that he covered by shaving his head bald, Libby's father hadn't changed. He was still imposing as hell. The gleam of the florescent lights off his scalp only highlighted the fact that at fifty-five, he was still nearly seven feet of solid muscle.

"Mr. Pruitt," Burke said with a tight smile. "I thought we agreed I would handle this—"

"No, I requested you inform me when you would be meeting with these men," Pruitt said.

"I thought it would be better if we handled this as quickly and quietly as possible."

Pruitt shook his head. "This is too important for me to handle by proxy. Now will you excuse us?"

The lawyer snapped his briefcase shut with definitive

clicks and stood. "I feel as if I have to go on record as saying both Libby and I think this is a *vast* overreaction."

"Noted," Pruitt said. "You're dismissed."

Aiming a scowl at the colonel's back, Burke yanked open the door and left the small room.

Pruitt crossed to stand in front of Jude. The man's dark blue eyes took in Jude's faded jeans, beat-up Nikes, and USMC hooded sweatshirt in one long, assessing sweep. "Lieutenant Wilde."

"Colonel." Jude resisted the instinct to salute. As an Officer Candidate struggling through OCS, he'd looked up to this man who had been one of his instructors at the time. Now all he felt toward Elliot Pruitt was an abyss of resentment, and he'd be damned before he showed the colonel one ounce of respect. "Didn't ever expect to see you again."

"Unfortunately, it was unavoidable in this situation."

Okay, this was bad. Ten minutes ago, Jude would've bet his balls that Pruitt would never voluntarily seek him out. Only something earth-shattering would mobilize the colonel into doing so. "What situation? What's going on?"

Pruitt drew a breath through his nose and squared his wide shoulders as if fortifying himself. "Libby's in trouble. She needs protection, and as much as it pains me to admit this, you're the best man for the job." The last was said with a faint sneer.

Jude ignored the flutter in his chest. It wasn't worry. Just…indigestion. Right. "What kind of trouble is she in?"

"She has a stalker, and the threats are getting more and more personal. We believe someone is trying to get her to drop the charges against Richard 'K-Bar' Niles."

"The gangbanger up for murdering that single mother in

Anacostia?" Camden asked.

Pruitt gave one curt nod of acknowledgment in the twins' general direction. "Yes. Libby's the prosecuting attorney, and of course, she's not going to drop it. The case is rock solid, but the trial isn't set to begin until August, and K-Bar made bail. He's free, and if he's not personally terrorizing her, then he's hired someone to do it for him."

"So you want to hire her some protection," Greer concluded.

"I want to hire *him*." Pruitt tipped his head toward Jude. "He and Libby have a history that will make it all that much easier for him to protect her. His sudden reemergence in her life won't raise any eyebrows."

Jude stared at his former instructor, fury burning hot in his gut. "You want me to pretend to be her lover? Like none of the past shit happened and we got back together?"

"It's a plausible reason for you to be around her all the time."

"No." Dread coiled its greasy fingers around his throat and squeezed. "No, no, no."

Pruitt paid no attention to his protests. "If you agree to my terms," he said to Greer, "he can start tomorrow morning."

"Do I really have to repeat my answer? How about, *hell* no? That sink in, Colonel?"

"This is not a request, Marine."

Jude got in Pruitt's face, his teeth clenched so hard his jaw ached. How dare the man ask this, after everything? He had some massive, steel-lined balls to come in here and dredge up a past Jude had spent eight years doing his damnedest to forget. "I'm not active duty. You can't order me around anymore. Sir."

Pruitt's rigid features softened—only the slightest bit, but Jude had seen that face screaming into his enough times that he noticed and backed off a step, his anger draining away. Sure, Elliot Pruitt was a hard-ass, in-it-for-life jarhead, but he wasn't a deadbeat father. His love for his only daughter was deeper even than his love for the Marines, and that was saying something. The strain he felt for her situation showed in the lines around his eyes. He just wanted her safe, and nobody could fault him for that.

"Find someone else," he told Pruitt softly and shook his head. "This plan? With me? Won't work."

"Yes, it will. I know the feelings you had for her, Wilde."

"*Had.* It was eight years ago, sir. People change."

"Not you." Pruitt jabbed a finger into his shoulder to enunciate each word. "Not about this."

What could he say to that? That he'd wanted the man's daughter more than he'd ever wanted anything? That he'd contented himself with a slew of nameless, faceless women who all blended together in his memory because none of them were the woman he loved? That he'd been noble one fucking time in his life and it had cost him more than anyone could imagine?

No. He had too much pride to admit all that, but any argument he made to the contrary would bounce off the colonel like a rubber bullet, so he kept his mouth shut. At his back, he could almost feel Camden twitching with eagerness to ask him about Libby Pruitt.

Greer shifted in his seat, and the springs of his chair squeaked as his two-hundred-thirty-pound, six-foot-five-inch frame reclined, breaking the silence. He folded his hands across his abs and studied Jude for a long moment, then sighed. "Give us a moment, Colonel? There's water and soda in the fridge out the door and to the left. Please, help yourself."

Pruitt gave a curt nod, nailed Jude with another stern look that was somehow a cross between an order and a desperate request, and then let himself out.

"I don't want to see her," Jude said once he was gone. "It's not fucking happening, Greer. Libby will castrate me if she sees me again. She won't go for the whole pretend relationship thing. Pruitt's out of his mind."

"What did you do to her?" Camden asked.

"The usual college romance sob story. Young love and all that, then I went and broke her heart in the worst way I knew how."

"You cheated," Greer concluded.

It took every ounce of control he had not to show his internal wince on his face. *Cheater*. Man, he hated that word, but he shrugged like it was all no big deal. Just Jude being his usual fuck up self. "And rubbed her face in it. I was young and stupid."

"You aren't still?" Reece asked.

Jesus. Sometimes he wished his second-oldest brother's snark came with a mute button. "We had something good, and I fucked it up. As usual. C'mon, you can't tell me you're surprised by that."

"No," Greer said. "I'm not."

Jude refused to let that answer sting. It was the truth, after all.

"How long were you with her?" Camden asked.

He thought about the ring in his pocket and considered

lying, because they sure as fuck wouldn't believe that he'd wanted to marry her more than he'd ever wanted anything in his life. He finally settled on a half-truth. "A year. I met her through Pruitt while at OCS." He still remembered the first time he saw her having lunch at a restaurant off base with her father. He'd approached them on the pretense of asking Pruitt a question, but he'd really just wanted to find out who the blond beauty in the strappy sundress and sandals was. "We dated during my senior year at Old Dominion and broke up after graduation, right after I was commissioned."

His brothers stared at him.

"No way," Camden said. "You've never stayed with anyone that long."

"Well, I did with her, okay?" Jude snapped. "And don't look at me like that. You all met her once at my apartment in Norfolk."

"Then why don't we remember her?" Greer asked.

"I do," Vaughn said.

"That's cuz you have the memory of an elephant," Cam said and elbowed his twin in the side.

"Pretty girl. Smart. Very sweet," Vaughn continued without missing a beat. "I thought she was too good for you."

"Yeah, I can't argue that." Jude dropped into the chair vacated by Pruitt's pretentious lawyer and rubbed both hands over his face. "When we were dating, I was always real careful about where we went, what we did, who we saw. Always took her out of town or to places where there was no chance of me being spotted with her."

"And why was that?" Reece asked, his tone full of disgust.

Because he'd wanted her to himself. He'd wanted her to know the real him and not the image he projected. And because he'd been warned away from her—several times. But his brothers didn't need to know any of that. "Because I didn't want this third degree."

Reece snorted. "More like you didn't want one of your other girlfriends to catch you."

"Yeah," Jude muttered and touched the ring in his pocket again. "You know me too well."

As his brothers processed the situation in silence, the dread tightening his chest started edging dangerously close to panic. He couldn't face Libby ever again. If it came to it, he wasn't sure he'd have the strength to hurt her a second time.

"So it's settled." He made sure there was no room in his tone for argument and got to his feet again, intent on making a quick escape. "I'm not doing it."

"No," Greer said. "You definitely are."

"*What?*"

"You always admit when you fuck up—I gotta give you credit for that—but you never really face your mistakes." Greer leveled that dark, all-too-knowing gaze on him and handed over the folder containing Libby's personal data. "It's long past time, bro, and after I hash out the details with Pruitt, you'll start tomorrow."

Chapter Two

"Late again."

"Dammit, I know." Libby Pruitt shoved into her office, hooked her purse over the back of her chair, and searched her desk drawers for a hair clip. Noah Saunders, her intern for the semester, lounged in the doorway, his skinny arms crossed over his chest. He already had a coffee stain on his tie, even though it was barely eight thirty, and his kinky, orange-red hair looked as if he had styled it with an explosion.

Unfortunately, he was the more organized out of the two of them this morning. Where was that damn clip? Despite her efforts, her hair was already out of control.

"You can't keep doing this," he said.

"Again, I know." Especially since her boss expected nothing less than 110 percent from his underlings. But it didn't help that her father seemed intent on making her life into a special kind of hell. With one ten-minute phone call, he'd managed to ruin her entire day before she'd even had her first cup of coffee.

Noah frowned. "You never used to be late for work. What's going on?"

Ah-ha. Hair clip. She twisted her hair into a ponytail and clipped it up. "We need to analyze the police reports regarding the Gatewood case—"

Noah straightened. He may have been a toothpick, but he was a tall toothpick and used his entire height to block her escape. "Libby, slow down a second. You can talk to me. Is something wrong?"

Her heart tripped, but she managed a smile she hoped didn't look as fake as it felt. "Of course not. It's just stress."

"Over K-Bar's release?"

Sure, she'd go with that. In a roundabout way, it was the truth. "He shouldn't have gotten out, and I feel somewhat responsible that he did."

"You did everything you could."

"Yes, but it wasn't enough. He's still free to terrorize people." One of those people being her, but she didn't mention that to Noah. He didn't need to know about the messages. The dolls. The disturbing voice mails. The distorted videos sent to her e-mail. Besides, she honestly didn't think K-Bar would try anything more than make scary, but idle, threats. She'd spent enough time studying him to know that if he'd wanted her dead, he would have convinced someone from his gang to get rid of her a long time ago. It would've been a quick, execution-style kill that she never would have seen coming.

So, no. K-Bar didn't want her dead. Of that, she was certain. He just wanted her terrified.

Now if only she could convince her dad of that. He was just compounding her stress by inviting a bodyguard into the mix—one he expected to play her boyfriend, of all crazy things.

"Libby?" Noah's hand passed in front of her face.

She blinked. "Sorry. What?"

"This zoning out… It isn't like you, either."

"I know." Shaking off her fears over her father's mental health, she bit her lower lip. "I'm okay. Really."

"If you're worrying about K-Bar walking, don't. Your case is airtight. He'll be back in jail before the end of summer. You got him," Noah said and offered a shy, goofy smile. "You're amazing."

Libby laughed and patted his arm. "I already told you, I'm too old for you."

His face flushed to a color that nearly matched his hair. "I-I didn't mean…"

"Joke. Relax." She gave his arm another pat, then ducked under it. Noah raced after her, stammering apologies for once again being unable to tell when she was joking with him.

"Noah, stop. It's fine. You have no need to apolo—" At the other end of the hall, a man stepped off the elevator with Kenneth, and her heart did a loop-de-loop. The stranger was around six one, his wide shoulders tapered into slim hips, and his jeans clung to his thighs as if they never wanted to let go. His dark hair was short on the sides and spiky on top, and she could just barely make out the ink of a tattoo on the side of his neck. Another peeked out from under the sleeve of a dark blue T-shirt. The shirt declared, "Trust me, I've done this before," in white letters. A wide, stainless steel hoop glinted from his earlobe as he nodded at something Kenneth said.

Earring? Tattoos?

Libby willed her heart to start beating again. Her imagination must be playing tricks on her, conjuring the image of the one person she thought about far too often but never wanted to see again, because for a moment, she thought this man was—

As if sensing her, he glanced up from his conversation and met her gaze with eyes the color of a cloudless morning sky. A flicker of unease passed over his expression before he gathered himself and straightened his shoulders as if preparing for battle. His dimples flashed, and the entirety of her existence flipped on its axis.

What. The. Hell?

Before she realized she was moving, she stalked down the hall and stopped in front of him. His grin only widened, and he snaked an arm around her waist, pulling her against all that hard muscle she remembered too well. He used to pull her in like this and kiss her every time he saw her, no matter if she had been gone for an hour or a week. It had made her feel special, wanted, adored.

What a crock.

"Hey, babe," he said with the same crooked half smile that at one time made her go all gooey-kneed. Except there was something different about him now, a tentativeness as he held her, a trait she'd never associated with him before. "I missed you."

She opened her mouth to tell him off—but his lips descended, hesitating only the barest of moments before lightly brushing hers. He lifted his head and stared into her eyes with an unreadable expression in his own. Then, with a groan, he drew her tighter against his body, and his lips dropped to hers again in an overwhelming, desperate kiss that crushed the last eight years into mere moments and short-circuited her mind with an electric pulse of sheer desire.

But she was…angry. Right? At him. Yes, the man who was currently rubbing his tongue over her bottom lip, seeking entrance, the man she didn't want to want—she should be furious at him right now. She just couldn't remember why as his kiss sizzled over her nerve endings and filled her head with white noise. God, did the man know how to use his lips or what? He always had, could always make the world melt away until she was nothing but a bundle of sensation.

Off to her left, Kenneth rudely cleared his throat, and the world snapped back into sharp focus.

Wait.

Babe?

Libby ripped away from the kiss and stared up into pale blue eyes rimmed with ridiculously long lashes. "Jude?"

His expression was a little dazed and his breathing ragged, but that didn't stop his gaze from dropping to her mouth. "Yeah?"

She rolled her hand into a fist, hauled it back, and punched Jude Wilde so hard the impact rung up her arm and into her own teeth. "Don't call me babe *ever* again."

The woman had a fist of steel.

Jude's head snapped back at the impact of Libby's

punch, and he was pretty sure he had cartoon Tweety Birds circling his noggin when he straightened. Even getting socked in the face by Vaughn, who expressed some of his more aggressive urges as a cage fighter, didn't rattle him half as much, but he'd long suspected his brother of pulling punches whenever they got into it.

Libby wasn't going to afford him that courtesy.

She balled up her fist like she planned to hit him again, but a giant matchstick, complete with the flame-red hair, stepped in front of her.

"Libby, stop!"

Burke sucked in a sharp breath through his nose. "Libby, what is wrong with you?"

She shook out her hand and drew a shuddering breath. Then, like nothing had happened, she straightened her suit jacket and turned on her heel. Matchstick spared Jude a confused glance before chasing after her.

Holy fucking ouch.

Jude worked his jaw. He'd be surprised if he didn't end up with a bruise as bad as the one Vaughn currently sported around his eye from yesterday's office rumble. "I thought Pruitt explained this charade to her?"

"He did," Burke said stiffly.

"Did he mention that I'm the guy he hired for the job?"

"It didn't come up."

"Of course not." Goddamn Pruitt. If he really loved his daughter so much, why would he spring this on her without preparing her first?

Burke paced the hallway, indignation seeping from his every pore. "I told Elliot this was a bad idea. We should have handled this on our own. We didn't need to bring in outsiders."

Jude didn't waste time with I-told-you-sos, even though he sorely wanted to say it. Maybe he was becoming a masochist, but now that he'd seen Libby again, and had tasted her, he couldn't leave without talking to her for real, no pretense.

And maybe one more taste.

Christ, that kiss. It should have been just a quick hello, a smooch from him playing the part of her lover. But once he felt her soft lips yield under his, he'd lost his fucking mind. He'd *needed* to kiss her.

So much for his acting skills.

He started down the hallway, intent on finding Libby and apologizing for the way her father blindsided her with him—but Burke caught his arm.

"Who are you to her?" Burke demanded. "Elliot won't tell me why he trusts *you* of all people to protect Libby."

The lawyer had the hands of a pansy, soft and thin, and Jude peeled those fingers from his arm with ease. "I could ask the same of you, GQ."

"We went to law school together." Burke sniffed, straightening the lapels of his suit coat. "We're friends."

Man, that uppity tone of his really grated on the nerves. "Friends. Aw, that's cute. I was her fiancé, so back off and let me do what Pruitt hired me to do."

Scowling, Burke backed up a step and then another. He kept backing away until he reached the elevator, then turned and jabbed the button.

Jude waited until Burke disappeared into the elevator before continuing down the hallway on his mission to apologize to Libby. The place was a maze of office doors. After two wrong turns and a set of ass-backward directions from a flirty brunette paralegal, he found her seated at her desk in her office, flipping through a stack of files. Matchstick stood beside her with a clipboard in hand and seemed to be taking notes.

Jude tried the doorknob. Nope. Locked. Damn.

Going with plan B, he tapped on the window with his knuckle. Matchstick looked up and scowled. Libby's shoulders stiffened, but she didn't lift her eyes from the papers on her desk.

Okay.

He doubled his fist and gave the lightly frosted glass a few good thumps. Matchstick, the flame-haired prick, positioned himself like a human shield between the door and the desk, then went back to note taking. Libby still didn't move.

Plan C then.

Jude grinned and started banging out a rocking drum solo on the window. Before he was even half way through "*Another One Bites the Dust*," Libby shoved away from her desk. By the time she twisted the lock and yanked open the door, an aura of pissed off all but sizzled the air around her. She had never looked hotter, and his cock took instant notice. Man, this woman could still turn him on like no other, and he wasn't sure how he felt about that.

She grabbed hold of his arm and dragged him into an empty conference room across the hall from her office.

"What grade are in you in?" she demanded as soon as the door clicked shut behind them. "Second?"

"Fifth. Never grasped the concept of long division and they kept holding me back."

"Unbelievable." She pushed out an exasperated breath.

"You're still the same asshole I know and hate."

"Whoa, now, Libs. Hate? That's a strong word."

"So is restraining order. Now are you finished?" She spun away and reached for the doorknob. "Because if you're done making a fool out of yourself, I'm going back to work."

Guilt left a bad taste in his mouth. As the woman he once loved to distraction, she deserved better than childishness from him. They were stuck in this less-than-ideal situation together, so why make it more difficult by being a jerk? The end of their relationship hadn't been her fault—that was 100 percent on his shoulders. And he was okay with that. Mostly.

He caught her hand. "Libs, wait."

"Don't call me that."

"Fine. Libby."

"Assistant District Attorney Pruitt to you."

His jaw tightened against the barb in her tone. Her coldness toward him shouldn't hurt. He deserved it and more. But, dammit, it did hurt. "All right, A.D.A. Pruitt, can we start over here?"

Her ponytail flopped as she shook her head. "Not possible."

"Why not?"

"Because you're…*you*."

Another barb, and it cut deeper than the first. "The fuck up."

"Yes. No." Sighing, Libby rubbed her eyes under her glasses with the fingers of one hand. "Jude, I'm not the girl I was eight years ago, okay?" Finally realizing he still held her other hand, she shook off his grip and reached for the door handle. "And I don't want any kind of relationship with you ever again."

Ouch.

No, he thought and touched the ring in his pocket to anchor himself, *not ouch*. This had been his goal when he hurt her—but that was supposed to have been all there was to it. Hurt her, move on with his miserable life without her, the end. He never would have guessed the whole nightmare of a situation would come back to bite him in the ass now.

Hand still on the doorknob, Libby stared at him over her shoulder as if she expected some kind of response to her declaration.

"Well," he said finally, "that's unfortunate, since your fatherhiredmetobeyourbodyguard-slash-pretend-boyfriend."

Did she just go pale? Maybe it was the harsh lighting in the conference room, but it sure looked like her complexion had lost a few shades of color when she spun back to face him. And, damn, there was that surge of guilt again. Even so, he couldn't tell her any of the whys because the truth would be much more painful than anything he'd done to her.

"W-what about the Marines?" she asked.

"Officially out a month ago."

"Oh."

"And seeing as we now have to convince everyone I'm your main man," he added after a beat of silence, "we need to learn to play nice with each other."

"Oh," she said again, apparently at a loss for words.

Another beat, longer this time.

"So," he prompted. "Can we start over?"

Libby chewed on her lower lip, naturally drawing his gaze to her mouth. Christ, the dreams he'd had about that mouth… He could still taste her, too, from his earlier attempt at playing his part, which didn't help dull the throb of need behind his fly. He remembered exactly how good it was between them and wanted that mouth on his again. And on other, lower portions of his anatomy.

"Meet me in the parking lot after work," she said finally, interrupting a particularly X-rated fantasy that had to do with her lipstick and his cock. "Jude, hello, did you hear me?"

"Er, right." He shook himself. "Parking lot. Gotcha."

"Five. Don't be late. I need to get home."

"Sure. See ya around." He gave a dorky half wave as she shook her head and opened the door. Cursing at himself, he stood in the empty conference room and shut his eyes.

See ya around?

Shit, maybe he *was* mentally stuck in the fifth grade. Where was his head?

Okay, dumb question. As soon as he'd seen Libby again, his brain had migrated south. She just looked so good, all curvy and womanly, and the fire in her eyes every time she looked at him…

Damn.

She'd always been fierce, but as a young college co-ed, she'd kept it carefully leashed and hidden behind a sweet exterior. At least until they hit the sack, and then she'd rock not only his world, but his whole freaking solar system. Adult Libby—now she was something else. She all but crackled with passion. Made a guy wonder…

And fantasize…

And lust…

Oh, man. He needed an ice bath, a-sap.

Chapter Three

"You're still here?" Libby stopped short in surprise when she exited her office to find Jude camped out on the floor beside her door, his long, jean-clad legs outstretched, his head tilted back against the tiled wall. His eyes were closed until she spoke, but he hadn't been sleeping. He thrummed with suppressed energy.

"Where else would I go?" he asked.

"How about away?"

Jude released a long breath. "Christ, woman, you really know how to hold a grudge."

"And you really know how to break a young girl's heart." He opened his mouth to reply, but she didn't want his excuses. She didn't care to think about the catastrophe that was their past, didn't know why she'd felt the need to bring it up, and shrugged as if it all meant nothing. "Just…forget it."

"For now," he said.

Lovely.

On his lap lay a closed folder, and she didn't have to strain to guess what it was: her dossier. She nodded toward it, desperate for a subject change. "Learn anything interesting?"

"Yeah." He smacked the folder against his palm and pushed to his feet. "You father is right to worry. You're not taking this threat seriously enough."

"C'mon. Not you, too. It's all harmless crap."

"It's escalating."

"That's bull."

"Go over everything for me," he commanded. "From the beginning. When did it all start?"

She faced him as disbelief roared through her. "You can't be serious."

"I rarely am, but in this case…"

"Well, I don't want to talk about it. You and Dad are worked up about nothing, and I refuse to give this…stalker… one nanosecond more of my time."

"Fuck me," Jude said. "Some things never change, huh? You're still so freakin' stubborn, knocking my head against a wall would be more productive than talking to you."

She conjured up her sweetest smile and waved a hand at the wall. "Knock yourself out. Please."

Jude scowled. "Libs—"

Her heart clenched. "Don't. You lost your right to use cutesy nicknames eight years ago."

With a heavy sigh that moved his wide shoulders, he corrected himself. "A.D.A. Pruitt, I need to hear the whole story from you. Your version, not some watered-down—or trumped-up—report."

Sure, now he had to go and be all reasonable.

"All right." She hitched the strap of her purse higher on her shoulder and started walking. She didn't wait to see if he was following. He was. He even had the audacity to reach out and take her hand. She tried to pull away, but he only tightened his fingers.

Okay then. If he really wanted to go through with this ridiculous charade, she could manage it as far as the parking lot.

"It started about a month ago," she explained. "Right after K-Bar made bond. Little things, at first, like a paper doll under my car's windshield wiper. I just brushed it off, but then the dolls started showing up with fewer clothes. Then with no clothes. Then the letters started."

"What did they say?"

"Things like 'see me now?' and 'I'm here.'" A chill clawed through her at the memory, despite her best efforts to repress it. "The worst was 'I'm waiting for you.' Then I started getting phone calls on my cell and videos sent to my e-mail. Always a distorted voice saying the same types of things as the notes."

"And the videos?"

They stepped into the elevator, and she hit the button for the ground floor. After the doors slid shut, she tried to pull her hand away from his. He held on and gave her a smile that was all challenge.

Giving up on the possibility of getting her hand back, she answered his question. "Same voice, but the picture is usually of a paper doll or blacked out. I saved them all if you want to see them. The first video frightened me enough that I finally told my father about it, and he overreacted and hired you."

"I don't think he overreacted."

Yeah, he wouldn't. For as different as Jude and her father were, in some ways they were very much the same. The elevator dinged, and the doors opened to the lobby, which she always thought looked more like the waiting area of a dentist office than a government building.

"Do you agree that the threats are from this gangbanger you're going to put away?" Jude asked.

"They're not threats," she told him.

"What would you call them then?"

"Not threats. None of them are overtly hostile. Just… creepy. If I took this to a courtroom and named them threats, the defense would hand me my ass on a silver platter."

"But do you agree with the possibility of K-Bar's involvement?" Jude persisted.

"Yes. He's trying to frighten me. He has been from day one. I had to get a restraining order against him to stop him from harassing me from prison."

Jude fell silent for a moment, his brows drawn together in an expression of concentration that was so very familiar. "Maybe," he said finally.

She sighed in exasperation. "Well, if not K-Bar, who else would it be?"

He shrugged one shoulder. "You do kinda have a knack for pissing people off."

"And you don't?"

"Hey, I didn't say it was a flaw. It's a knack. A propensity. No, a forte. That's a good one. *Forte*." He exaggerated the accent on the word and let go of her hand long enough to hold open the building's front door. As soon as they were both through, his hand found hers again. "I want you to make up a list of other possible suspects that I can give to my brothers for background checks."

"That's not necessary. They don't need to waste their time."

"Nah, Reece's only pleasure comes from running background checks. God knows the dude has no life to speak of."

A cloud of dust danced across the pavement, and clouds lumbered toward the city from the east, dark and foreboding, promising a storm. The gusty, late spring wind still held enough of a hint of winter that it ripped the heat from her body, but with Jude's hand encircling hers, she didn't feel the chill. That hand, so familiar and yet so different, rougher with more calluses than she remembered… It could give pleasure like she hadn't felt since he last touched her.

Too bad it wasn't attached to a different man.

As if sensing the direction of her thoughts, he stopped walking and turned her bodily to face him. He'd done a lot of growing up in these last eight years. When she met him in college, he'd still been handsome in the way of a teenager, wholesome and fresh-faced. Now, no trace of that twenty-two-year-old boy remained in his chiseled jaw, wide shoulders, and shadowed pale blue eyes. He towered over her, making her feel petite when she hadn't qualified as petite since middle school. At five eight, she was constantly fighting a battle against her size-ten jeans, and more often than not, she lost due to long hours at the office, lots of on-the-go food, and no time for a daily workout. She had wide-load hips and D-cup boobs and never thought of either as sexy—until Jude looked at her with that hot gleam in his eyes.

God, why couldn't he have gained a hundred pounds and lost all his teeth in the last eight years? She hated that she was still attracted to him.

"Fearless Libby," he said in such a low tone that she almost couldn't hear him over the wind. She saw the kiss coming. Could have avoided it, but dammit, she wanted it. Wanted to know if having his mouth on hers was as erotic as it had been earlier when he'd kissed her in the hallway.

He dragged his lips over hers, back and forth, back and forth, a barely there caress that lit her up from the inside like a human torch. It wasn't fair how her body responded instantly to him when she'd spent years having to coax even a mild reaction from it. After Jude devastated her life, sex had become a chore rather than a pleasure, and she'd taken to avoiding even the most casual of encounters. And now here he was again, offering part of what she'd once had. Offering what she burned for, what she shouldn't still want.

She nipped at his lip, punishing him for making her ache with desire like this, but he didn't back away. Instead, he took that as an invitation, and the taste of him filled her mouth as he invaded and claimed. She gripped his shoulders, needing the rock-solid weight to steady herself. Her head roared with a jumbled mix of outrage and don't-you-dare-stop.

No, wait. That roaring sound wasn't her head. A…car?

Jude yanked away with a curse, and before she fully grasped what was happening, he folded his body into a protective shield around her and spun them to the left. She felt a jarring thump as Jude took the brunt of their landing and heard him grunt in pain, but he didn't let go of her as they rolled across the pavement. The car with the noisy engine whipped past in a flash of blue and a squeal of tires as it fishtailed out of the lot.

"Damn," Jude breathed and helped her to her feet

again. Her knees wobbled. He steadied her with a hand on her shoulder. "You okay, Libs?"

"Yes," she said, eying him up and down. He had a tear in the thigh of his jeans and seemed to be favoring his right side. "Are you? Did it hit you?"

"No. Landed hard, but I'm fine." He grinned. "Better than fine. This is the most fun I've had in weeks. Feels good to get the adrenaline going. Wanna have sex?"

Libby huffed out a breath in disbelief. "You're insane."

"Depends on your definition. So is that a no?"

"Yes."

His eyes danced. "Yes?"

"No! I meant yes as in yes, it's a no. I mean—" She threw up her hands. She never got tongue-tied, and yet she couldn't seem to string two coherent sentences together around him. But at least she could stand on her own two feet now without wobbling, and she had a sneaky suspicion he'd put her on the defensive for just for that reason. "I'm going home."

"Good." All the laughter faded from his expression. "Nobody can try to run you over there."

"What?" She stared up the street where the car had disappeared. "You think that was on purpose?"

"Yeah, I do. Did you recognize the car? It was meant for you because as far as I know, nobody's out to kill me."

"If they *knew* you, they would be," she said between her teeth. "It was just an accident, Jude. I've never seen that car before. It wasn't aiming for me."

"Twenty dollars says you're wrong."

"All right."

He pointed to something over her shoulder. Dread turned her stomach sour as she spun and stared at the windshield of her Subaru Impreza.

WATCH OUT.

The words screamed at her in blood-red paint, and a nude paper doll had been stuck to the trailing line off the T like an obscene exclamation point.

"No." She swayed again, and Jude slid an arm around her waist to steady her.

His expression hardened, and he all but dragged her toward a black truck parked three spaces down from her car. He opened the passenger-side door and lifted her into the seat. Numb, she stared at the dashboard, barely noticing when he climbed into the driver's side and started the engine.

Someone was actually trying to kill her.

Holy hell.

"We got a problem," Jude said.

She glanced over to lash out with a derisive, "No shit, Sherlock." Not very original as far as comebacks went, but she wasn't exactly at the top of her game.

Except he wasn't speaking to her. He held a phone to his ear.

"An attack," he added. "There was another message on her car. Yeah, another doll, too. Then someone tried to run us down with a blue four-door sedan, possibly a late-model Ford Taurus. I got a partial plate number." After that, whoever was on the other end of the line did most of the talking. He nodded once, then again, then said, "Okay," before hanging up.

"Who was that?"

He slid the phone back into his coat pocket. "Your father. He's going to meet us at your place."

"Oh. Great." Here she'd thought this day couldn't *possibly* get any worse, and now she had to deal with Jude and her overbearing, overprotective father at the same time. "I thought you two hated each other."

"We're Marines. Personal feelings don't factor into missions."

"Missions. Right. I'm just another mission." She told herself not to let that hurt and failed miserably. The dispassionate tone he'd used burrowed under her skin and tweaked at her nerves. She angled her head at him. "Personal feelings don't factor into anything for you, do they? You avoid emotion like leprosy."

"Pretty much. Emotion is messy."

She slumped in back in her seat. The jabs she kept taking at him weren't wholly deserved, especially after he saved her from becoming a road pancake, but she just couldn't seem to help herself. The man pushed all of her buttons—good and bad—and right now, she needed the distraction he presented. Anything to take her mind off the image of that car headed directly toward them…

Oh God, why wouldn't her hands stop shaking?

She rolled her fingers into fists on her lap and clenched her jaw to keep the trembles from traveling up her arms and into the rest of her body.

For once, Jude didn't rise to the bait of her snide remarks. He studied her for a second, then reached over and covered both of her hands with one of his.

"Jesus, your hands are half-frozen."

She tried to pull away, but his grip tightened. She wasn't going anywhere until he allowed it, and that knowledge grated. "Let go of me."

To her surprise, he did and turned up the heat, angling the vents her way. But, being Jude, he couldn't leave it at that. "You used to like when I touched you."

She still did, a little thrill dancing through her belly at every contact, but she'd bite off her own tongue before admitting it. "I was young, stupid, and horny back then."

One corner of his mouth kicked up in a half smile. "Yeah, been there."

"From what I've seen, you're still there," she said.

He actually laughed. "You know, Reece said the same thing to me yesterday. Sure he's not *your* brother?"

She vaguely remembered Reece and Greer. And the twins, but she couldn't remember their names. She'd met them all once at Jude's apartment, but only very briefly. Jude had rushed through the introductions and then hurried his brothers out the door, making a fake excuse about having dinner reservations.

That should have been her first clue their relationship was doomed.

Young, stupid, and horny.

She looked at him again, let her eyes trace the line of his long, muscled frame, and a spark of pure desire heated her from the inside out.

Yeah, so what was her excuse for wanting him now?

When Jude pulled to the curb in front of her house, her father's car already waited in the driveway, and he stood in the open doorway, his big body backlit by the lamps in the living room. He held a gun in his hand.

Libby sighed and got out of Jude's truck. "Dad, put that away."

He merely grunted.

"Daddy, please. You're overreacting."

With the tip of his gun, he pulled her front door shut. "Is *this* overreacting?"

"Shit," Jude said from behind her.

Heart in her throat, she stared at the streaks of dark red splattered over the door. Here, too? No, not here. Not at her home, her sanctuary from the world. "Is that…?"

"Paint," her father said. "Now come inside out of the open."

"Oh." Relief shook her to the bone. Her legs didn't seem to want to move. "Paint. Right. Just…paint."

"Wilde."

"Yes, sir," Jude said, and suddenly her feet were no longer touching the ground. She wanted to tell him to put her down, that she could walk herself, thank you very much, but her vocal cords had also stopped cooperating. Jude carried her into the house.

How ironic, she thought. Here he was, finally carrying her over the threshold after all these years. Tears threatened, and she focused on blinking them back. She must be an emotional wreck right now if something as ridiculous as an old romantic fantasy brought on the waterworks.

"Plan B," her father said.

"I didn't know we had one," Jude responded and set her down on her favorite overstuffed leather recliner.

"We do now." Her father tucked a chenille throw around her shoulders, and she clutched it, welcoming the warmth. "You have to take her away from the city. Hide her somewhere, keep her safe until the trial."

"How far are you thinking?" Jude asked.

"I own a hunting cabin in the mountains in Vermont—"

"No." Jude moved away from her, over to one of the three front windows. He nudged the curtain aside and peeked out as if he expected her stalker to be across the street, watching…waiting…

Oh God.

Libby buried her face in her hands.

"Why the hell not?" her father demanded. "The cabin's defensible, remote. A perfect place to hide."

"Yeah, until a storm blows in and strands us up there with a psycho killer. Haven't you ever seen a horror movie?" When her father said nothing in response, Jude let the curtain fall and turned back to them. "You don't want her trapped someplace all alone. Sure, she might be harder to find, but once she's found, she has no way of getting help fast. You want her someplace well populated, someplace where the locals see new faces every day and don't question it."

"And you have such a place in mind?"

"One or two," Jude said, and the undercurrent of laughter in his voice finally snapped Libby out of her fog.

Wait. They wanted to take her out of the city?

"Stop." She shook off the blanket and stood. "Don't I get a say in this?"

"No," they said at the same time, and in that moment, the similarities between the two men struck her speechless—except one meant everything to her and the other she wanted nothing to do with.

She turned to the only one who mattered. "I'm not going

anywhere, Dad."

His expression softened, and he soothed down a flyaway strand of her hair. "You don't have a choice, sweet pea. Whoever this is knows where you live. I won't take a chance with my only daughter's life."

"And I understand that, but you can't just ship me off somewhere. I'll get a hotel."

"Not good enough. You need protection."

All right. If that was how he wanted to play it, she could be stubborn, too. She was her father's daughter after all. She crossed her arms over her chest and lifted her chin. "Then hire someone else because I'm not going anywhere with *him*."

Her father looked at Jude for a long moment, then back at her. "He saved your life tonight."

"Yes." And did that mean she owed him something? Because she really didn't want to be indebted to Jude Wilde in any way. She could only imagine his version of a repayment plan. "But I can't stand him. He's selfish, hedonistic, reckless, and…and I don't want to be near him."

Jude grinned. "You're full of compliments."

She propped a hand on her hip and held her other out as if to say, *see what I mean?*

"Yes, he is all those things," her father agreed with a long-suffering sigh. "And he can't take an order for shit, but he's also good at what he does, the best I've ever had the misfortune to train. He'll keep you safe for me."

Oh no, this couldn't be happening. Frantic, she searched for another excuse. "I can't leave my job."

"I already talked to your boss. He said you have plenty of vacation time coming and agrees that you should take it.

Please, Elizabeth," he added softly. "Please. For me."

She studied his face, noted the new lines around his weary eyes. "You're really worried about this, aren't you?"

"Very. You should be, too, and it terrifies me that you're not."

Closing her eyes, she let out a breath in defeat. There would be no winning this battle, and honestly, she wasn't sure she even wanted to. Elliot Pruitt never admitted to such weaknesses as worry or fear. That he would do so now only went to show exactly how concerned he was.

"All right." She took a moment to fortify herself before she faced Jude. "What should I pack?"

The man grinned, and tendrils of heat curled through her belly at the sight of his dimples. Damn him.

"Swimsuit," he said.

"Figures."

As she stalked toward her bedroom, she heard him laugh. This was going to be one long, headache-inducing vacation.

Chapter Four

The house was exactly the way he remembered it: smack dab in the middle of the city and completely secluded behind a stone fence and a lush tropical garden.

Perfect place to hide from the world.

Jude pulled up to the gate at the backside of the property and leaned out his open window to wave at the camera. As he waited for the gate to slide open, he glanced over at Libby, asleep in the passenger seat. Her hair was loose for the first time since their reunion. A sudden, visceral memory all of that sleek gold spread across his thighs as she did the most amazing things to his body with her mouth hit him hard in the gut and made his jeans painfully tight.

And yet he couldn't look away. He'd missed seeing her like this, completely relaxed, her defenses down. Somehow, she looked smaller when she slept, and he wanted to wrap himself around her, shield her from all the bad in the world. No other woman aroused that protective instinct in him like

Elizabeth Pruitt, and it was irritating as hell.

Damn, she was still as gorgeous as she'd been in college — maybe even more so now because her body had curves it had lacked back then. Lush, intriguing curves that had tormented him during the entire flight to Florida. Thanks to her reclined position, her baggy T-shirt pulled tight across her chest and showcased her bigger breasts. What he wouldn't give to see those babies bare as she sat astride him, riding him hard until they both came screaming.

Fuck.

Annoyed and uncomfortable, Jude shoved open the rental's door and slid out. Why was he torturing himself with something he'd never have again? He'd burned that bridge to ashes eight years ago, and there would be no crossing back over it. So he needed to chill with the X-rated fantasies.

Leaning against the hood of the car, he jingled the ring in his pocket and took a moment to enjoy the warm night air, fragrant with salt, sand, and flowers he couldn't begin to name. Someone played a guitar nearby, and the dulcet tones of the song soothed over him like a lover's caress.

Ah, Key West. He'd missed it here, hadn't been back since his very short visit last year. He winced at the memory as a figure stepped into the splash of his rental's headlights. A vice tightened in Jude's chest, but he plastered on an easy smile and faced the house's owner.

"Hey, Seth." He walked slowly toward the gate, hands held in plain view at his sides, the poster boy of nonthreatening. Even though he'd called ahead and his arrival had been expected, he didn't dare make any sudden moves.

Last time he'd seen Seth Harlan... Well, it had ended badly. He'd thought that after his best friend's experience overseas, a friendly face would do him good, help him heal or some shit, so he'd traveled to Key West as soon as Seth was stateside. But he'd been wrong. The mere sound of his voice had sent Seth hurtling into a flashback. The guy had smashed a beer bottle, then threatened everyone in the bar with the shards of glass. After that, as much as it had killed Jude to keep his distance, he'd stayed away.

Until now.

Christ, first Libby and now Seth. All the skeletons from his past were rattling to life this week.

"Been a long time. How you doin'?" he asked. The guy had lost a lot weight and no longer resembled the muscular man Jude remembered from their days of raising hell together on and off base. "You holdin' up?"

"Working at it." Seth's voice sounded rusty, like he never used it, and his gaze was a little wild as it bounced from Jude to the car, where Libby slept in the passenger seat. "That the woman?"

"Yeah, that's Libby. You remember me talking about her during OCS, don't you?"

A ghost of a smile drifted across Seth's lips. "You wouldn't shut up about her." The smile disappeared. "Then one day you wouldn't talk about her at all."

"Shit happens, people drift apart."

"I know. Believe me. And yet here she is with you." He stared at the ground. "I'd be lying if I said I wasn't jealous you got her back."

Jude winced. "Yeah, I was sorry to hear about Emma calling off the engagement like that. You two were great together."

Seth raised one shoulder in a halfhearted shrug, then

unlocked the chain on the gate and pulled one side open. "She's better off. I'm…not right anymore, ya know?"

After what he went through in Afghanistan, Jude thought, *who would be?* Nobody came back from that kind of torture in one piece.

"But," Seth added with steel in his tone, "I'm gonna get right."

Jude couldn't help it, he strode forward and embraced the man who was once his best friend in a hard, backslapping hug. "Nah, man, you're golden. You're a walking miracle, and I am so fucking happy to see you back in the world."

Behind them, the car door opened. "Jude?" Libby said.

"Hey, you're awake. Come on over here and meet one of the best men I know. Libby, Seth Harlan. He's lending us his house."

Libby nodded and held out a hand. "Thanks for letting us stay here."

"It's no problem." After only the slightest hesitation, Seth accepted the handshake. "I won't be around, and I feel better knowing someone else will be. Speaking of…" He fished in the pocket of his hoodie and produced a ring of keys that he handed to Jude. "You remember where every-thing is?"

"Sure do."

"All right then." Seth grabbed a rucksack that sat propped against the edge of the stone fence and slung it over his shoulder. "I have a…plane…to catch." He said the word "plane" in the same tone other people used for "cockroach."

Jude squeezed his shoulder in a show of support. "You'll be fine. I've been hearing nothing but good things about HORNET. Vaughn went through BUD/S with the two guys heading the team, and he says they'll take care of you. Do you need a lift to the airport?"

"No." He drew a breath, gazed up and down the street, and then pulled up the hood of his sweatshirt. "I'll walk."

Jude recognized that action for what it was—a defense mechanism, a way to hide from the world—and suddenly he wasn't so sure about letting Seth go it alone. "You sure?"

"I need to walk," Seth corrected himself and hitched the pack up into a better position on his shoulders. "I have to prove to myself…yeah. I just have to."

Jude tried for a smile. "Man, you always did have more balls than brains. Probably the reason we got along so well."

"That hasn't changed." He started down the drive but paused at the sidewalk and turned back. "Hey, Wilde, I never blamed you for what happened to me. When I get home, let's grab a beer. Catch up."

The lump that formed in Jude's throat made speaking impossible, so he just nodded and lifted his hand in a salute. Seth returned the salute with a smile. Then, after another moment of hesitation, he stepped out onto the sidewalk and headed toward a second chance at life.

Christ knew he deserved it.

Jude watched the empty sidewalk until fingers brushed his wrist. He glanced down to see Libby staring at him with an unreadable expression on her face.

"Your friend is a strange one," she said.

Jude shook off her hand and strode to the car. "You have no idea the hell he's been through."

She waited until he pulled the car into the driveway, then shut and locked the gate. "I didn't mean to offend you."

"Well, you did." He slammed the door and went to the

trunk to grab their bags, but she caught his arm before he could stomp off into the house like he wanted.

"I'm sorry."

He spun on her. "After what happened to that man, he could've just said the hell with it and put a bullet in his brain. But he didn't. He's got a job with a private hostage rescue team, he's pulling his life back together. He's stronger than any man I know and deserves nothing but your respect."

"I-I really am sorry. I didn't know."

Of course she didn't know. Damn. Feeling like a heel, he shut his eyes and tried exhaling his irritation. After spending his entire day camped out on the floor in front of her office, then yanking her out of the way of that car, followed by the plane ride to Florida, his entire body was one big throb and his eyes felt like he'd scoured them with gravel. And that was before the emotional humdinger of seeing Seth again.

What he needed was to get unpacked and take a nice, long soak in the hot tub.

"Let's get inside," he said. "I'll show you the house."

"Okay." She held out a hand for her bag, but he ignored it. Not because he wanted to be a gentleman, but because his muscles had stiffened up. The less unnecessary movement he engaged in, the better. He tilted his head, indicating a stone path lit with solar lanterns. He'd deal with pulling the car into the two-bay garage later. "This way."

"It's beautiful," Libby said after they'd traveled several feet into the garden. The path dumped them out next to the in-ground pool, and she stopped to stare. "Wow."

Jude also paused to take in the view, remembering his own similar reaction when, fresh out of Officer Candidates School, he'd first visited this place. The pool was long enough to swim laps and glowed an inviting blue from the underwater lighting tucked along the edges. An overhang of tropical trees provided shade during the day and gave it the feel of a hidden oasis.

Tons of fond memories here. Seth's house had been the hotspot whenever he and his Marine buddies got an extended leave. Lots of barbecues, all-nighter parties, women, and drunken good times had happened here over the years.

Part of him missed it all.

Jude crossed the concrete pool deck to the open-air seating area, passed the covered pool table and comfortably padded wicker furniture arranged around a slate fire pit, and opened the French doors into the kitchen.

Libby followed and sucked in a surprised breath. "This is not what I expected when you said 'safe house.' Does Seth live here by himself?"

"Yeah." He set their bags down by the island counter and studied the house's open floor plan. The place looked less like the bachelor pad it used to be and more like a showroom example of snazzy Key West real estate. Seth had bought new furniture in a creamy off-white leather and had painted the living room walls a bright red-orange. For christs-sakes, the striped pillows on the couches even matched the color of the walls exactly.

Man, Seth had way too much time on his hands.

"He must be wealthy to afford a place like this in Key West," Libby said and ran her hand over a baby grand piano, which matched the color of the furniture.

"Inheritance," Jude said. "His father's a big wig in the agricultural industry in Iowa. Seth's always had money to burn. This used to be his family's vacation house until his father bought a place in the Virgin Islands. Then Seth took it over and used it as a crash pad when he was on leave."

"I love the windows, the colors… It's all so cheerful."

Jude didn't mention that if she had spent a year as a prisoner of war, she'd need to surround herself with light and color. Instead, he just picked up their bags again and stifled a groan. He needed to get into the bedroom and change into his swim trunks. That hot tub was all but screaming his name.

"Well, this is it," he said. "Kitchen here, living room there. That little room by the piano's an office area. Bedroom's down this hallway, first door. Second door's a gym. Third is the laundry room." He hitched a thumb behind him at the short hallway beside the galley kitchen. "Bedroom has an en suite, and there's a half bath off the living room." As he spoke, he headed toward the bedroom, moving as fast as he dared. "Home sweet home for a while."

In the master suite, he tossed the bags on the king-size bed, which took up most of the available space, and started to strip off his shirt. A ball of orange fur yowled and scampered out from under the bed and between his legs, nearly knocking him over.

Cat.

Christ, why didn't Seth mention a cat? Not that he had anything against the animal, but a little warning would have been nice. Feeling bad for scaring the poor thing, he squatted down. Except how did you call a cat?

He snapped his fingers. "Here kitty, kitty."

Libby appeared in the doorway, the enormous animal purring like a motorboat in her arms as she scratched at its head. "That doesn't work. Besides, his name is Sam."

"How do you know?"

"Seth left a note on the counter in the kitchen. Plus, it says so on his collar. Uncle Sam."

Right. 'Cuz what else would Seth name his cat?

Jude stood, unzipped his bag, and dug around until he found his swim trunks. "You know how to take care of that beast?"

"It's not rocket science. Cats are mostly self-sufficient."

"Good. Then he's your responsibility. I have enough to worry about."

"Humph." Scratching the fur ball under its chin, she wandered over to the floor-to-ceiling windows overlooking the pool and garden, and damn, he liked the way those yoga pants she was wearing clung to her curves, highlighting every sway of her hips. He could imagine peeling her out of them, exposing all the soft female skin of her thighs. Sometimes, in his weaker moments, he could still feel that skin, those thighs wrapped around his hips as he surged into her body and—

"Is this the only bedroom?" she asked.

Oh fuck. This was going to be a long mission if he kept up this kind of reminiscing. He made himself look away from her ass. "Yup."

"So...where I am supposed to sleep?"

"You have two choices. We share the bed or you can have the couch."

She whirled around and glared at him, but it was hard to look intimidating with a giant orange cat in your arms, and he told her so. She flipped him the bird, which lightened his mood considerably. Bantering he could handle, and it took his mind off the half-hard state of his cock.

"A gentleman would give up the bed," she said, all prim and proper.

"Pretty sure we established a long time ago that I'm no gentleman." He waggled his brows at her, just to see what kind of reaction he'd get. "And I know for a fact the bed's big enough for at least four people."

"You *would* know that, wouldn't you?"

"What, you think I was celibate after we ended?"

She huffed out a disgusted breath and stalked from the room with the cat still purring in her arms. Well, that was one way to get her to go away.

Now about that hot tub.

Chapter Five

"What did I ever see in him?" Libby asked the cat as she stomped back to the living room. "Men are complete assholes, you know that?"

Sam mewed in a surprisingly gentle voice for such a big guy, and she rubbed him under the chin.

"Oh, not you," she cooed. She'd always wanted a pet and had a particular fondness for cats, but didn't think it was fair to keep an animal when she was barely home long enough to catch a full eight hours of sleep. "You're a sweet boy, aren't you?"

"Why, yes, I am."

She whirled as Jude stepped out of the bedroom wearing nothing but a pair of board shorts and a towel draped over one shoulder. Holy…abs. And pecs. Flat copper nipples puckered in the air-conditioned room. A soft line of dark hair arrowed downward from his navel, pointed to the low-slung waistband of his shorts.

This could not possibly be the same man she'd dated all those years ago. He'd been in decent shape back then, but in a skinny runner kind of way—nothing like this. His extra wide shoulders narrowed into a sharp V at his hips, where a tribal swirl peeked out over the edge of his shorts. Muscle roped his chest, and a phoenix tattoo took flight on his arm, so large that the tips of its fiery wings reached toward his ear. She itched to run her fingers over it, as appreciative of the amazingly artistic design as of the bicep it decorated.

"That's a lot of tattoos," she said, then could have kicked herself for it. Nothing like letting him know she'd been looking.

"So what? I like getting inked."

"I don't mind." When he looked at her sharply, she fumbled. "I mean, uh, I like the phoenix on your arm. When did you have it done? I thought the Marines have a strict policy about tattoos not showing under their PT gear."

"They do." His expression softened. "I had it done the week after I got out. I've spent the last month getting the ink I wanted but couldn't have before. Next I have plans for a sleeve."

"Well…" Her mouth went dry. She should not find the idea of a tattoo sleeve at all sexy—but she did. Oh boy, did she ever, and she couldn't help but imagine what it'd feel like to trace all of those inked designs with her tongue…

Jude was staring at her hard, as if waiting for something.

"Oh." She fumbled for words, realizing she'd been lost in her forbidden fantasies. "I just wanted to tell you they're all beautiful, but that phoenix is a work of art."

He reached out and brushed his knuckles over her cheek in a shockingly tender caress. "It reminds me of you.

The colors, the spark…"

"Me?" She gave a nervous laugh and backed up a step. She hugged the cat to her chest like a shield. "That's not me. You must have me confused with one of your other women."

"My other women. Yeah," he scoffed, and all hints softness in his expression disappeared. Her calculated barb had hit its mark, but she refused to feel bad for it when it was the truth.

Jude grumbled something under his breath and continued toward the sliding patio doors. He seemed to be moving more stiffly than before, his once graceful walk stilted as if he were trying not to limp.

Jeez. With everything else that had happened, she'd all but forgotten he'd hit the ground hard when he pulled her out of the way of that car. His body was probably one giant throb of pain right now, and he hadn't said so much as "ow" in complaint.

"Are you okay?"

"Will be."

"Do you need anything?" She didn't want to be concerned, but couldn't help the note of worry that crept into her voice. Especially when he turned to look at her and she caught sight of the bruises coloring his right leg a deep purple.

"Aw, Libs. Are you worrying over me?"

The cat wiggled, and she set him down. Her arms felt empty and awkward now that she didn't have Sam to hold, and she wasn't sure what to do with them. She finally crossed them over her chest. "You were almost hit by a car. I would be heartless not to worry a little."

"And you're definitely not that. If anything, you have too much heart."

Okay, that surprised her. Was he being sarcastic? He looked pretty damn serious, but she couldn't tell for sure. Before she could decide how to respond, he gave a smile half the wattage of his usual grin. "I just need a soak. Maybe a beer."

"Beer? You can't drink."

He lifted one brow. "Watch me."

"I mean, on the job. You can't drink while you're working."

"I'm a private investigator. I can do whatever the hell I want." When she scowled, he added more softly, "A beer or two is not going to prevent me from protecting you, and we're perfectly safe here. Nobody except Seth, my brothers, and your father know where we are. And Seth just thinks we're on our honeymoon."

Her stomach twisted at a sudden, painful memory she'd long since buried. He'd promised her this. *Exactly* this. The house tucked away in a tropical garden, the in-ground pool, the hot tub, Key West. The morning after he asked her to marry him, he'd promised to bring her here, to his friend's vacation house, one of his favorite places in the world, for their honeymoon. And she, foolish girl that she was, had drifted through her classes that day on a cloud of naive happiness, showing everyone her ring with its pathetic diamond, dreaming of the wedding, the honeymoon, their life together. By the time her friends took her out to celebrate that weekend, she'd had them living in wedded bliss in the suburbs with three kids, a dog, and a cat.

In fact, she'd been so blinded with love that she almost missed his betrayal entirely. Her friends tried to tell her when he walked into the club with another woman, but she brushed them off as jealous. It wasn't until her roommate had taken her by the arm and spun her around to face the bar, that she finally understood. Jude sat on one of the stools with a stunning brunette standing between his legs, her long body pressed as close to him as she could get with clothes on, and her tongue down his throat. Even then, with the evidence of his cheating staring Libby in the face, she hadn't wanted to believe it. She thought maybe this was some kind of misunderstanding or a case of mistaken identity like in the movies. But Jude lifted his head and looked right at her, his pale blue eyes cold. Heartless. Like he hadn't proposed to her only two days before.

Without a single word, she strode up to him and dropped the ring into his drink. Then she turned away, and as tears smeared her mascara and blurred her vision, she'd heard the brunette ask him who she was. His response killed every last tender feeling she might have harbored for him.

Nobody.

She was nobody to him.

He never tried to call, never offered any kind of excuse, lame or otherwise. He just vanished. She tortured herself for years, wondering what she'd done in the two days between his proposal and his betrayal to make him change his mind.

Libby shoved that all out of her thoughts. It didn't matter. It was like a previous conviction that couldn't be brought in front of the jury and had no bearing on their current situation.

Jude was still talking, oblivious to her trip down ugly memory lane, and she forced herself to focus on what he was saying.

"...my brothers are keeping an eye out for K-Bar, and Seth has this place wired up better than the CIA." He exhaled a hard breath and shook his head. "Guess some good came out of his paranoid psychosis after all."

And there was the perfect segue to ask the question that had been bothering her since Seth left. Plus, it had the added benefit of taking her mind off the past. The way he'd acted with Seth flew in the face of everything she thought she'd known about Jude Wilde.

"What did he mean when he said he doesn't blame you?"

"You know what? A beer or six sounds like an excellent idea." He detoured to the fridge and grabbed a six-pack out of the door. "Let's indulge. This is our honeymoon, babe."

"Don't call me babe." But she took one of the bottles he handed her and trailed him out to the patio. Watched as he pulled the cover off the hot tub and started the jets. He settled into the steaming water with a sigh, letting his head drop back against the padded side, and said nothing more for several long moments.

When she didn't go back inside, he lifted his head. "You gonna stand there all night or join me?"

God, she was tempted. It looked like a slice of heaven, but… No. Way too intimate.

She settled for sitting down on the edge and dipping her feet into the water. "So you're not going to answer me?"

"About what?" he mumbled, the question slurred like he was already half-asleep.

"About what Seth said."

He studied her, then took a long pull from his beer. "You're not gonna drop it, are you?"

"No."

"Well, shit. You can't think any worse of me." He drained the beer, his Adam's apple bobbing in his strong neck with each swallow. When he finished, he snagged another bottle.

"Slow down," she said. Considering they hadn't eaten dinner, she'd be scraping him off the bottom of the tub before long if he kept this up.

He ignored her, twisted off the cap, and tapped the neck against her bottle. "To friends."

"Okay." That was something she could definitely drink to. "Friends."

As she raised her beer to her lips, he added, "May they always cover your ass, even if it nearly gets them killed."

Oh, yes, there was a story here. She set her drink down without taking a sip. "What happened?"

Jude twirled the neck of his bottle between two fingers. "I was supposed to go on that mission, the one that… Fuck."

Libby waited, her instincts telling her that if she opened her mouth now, he'd use the opportunity to change the subject. Worse, he'd clam up, and she'd never find out what happened between him and Seth. For reasons she couldn't begin to name, it was important to hear the story.

"Seth wasn't supposed to go on the mission," Jude said softly after a long moment. "But he covered for me. I woke up that morning sick as hell. He was afraid I'd go out there and get myself or my men killed, so he took my place. Told our captain I had the flu." He gave a humorless laugh. "Turns out, he wasn't lying. The nasty food, shitty living conditions, and lack of sleep all combined into one helluva bug that kept me bedridden for a week. I ended up in the hospital in Germany with pneumonia, and I didn't find out for another week that they'd been ambushed. All but three of them died in the attack. Of those three, Seth's the only one who survived captivity."

Oh God. She couldn't begin to imagine… No, she decided. She didn't want to imagine what it must have been like for Seth. She couldn't help him, but Jude was another matter entirely. Sitting there in the tub, reliving the nightmare of discovering his best friend was a prisoner of war, he looked so worn down, nothing like his usual jovial self.

Unable to think of anything else to do to offer comfort, Libby reached out with her foot and touched her toes to his calf. He glanced up in surprise at the contact, and she made herself hold his gaze. "I can see why Seth doesn't blame you."

Jude snorted. "He should."

"Why? Did you mastermind the ambush?"

"Hell no."

"Did you purposefully get sick so you couldn't go on the mission?"

"Of course not."

"There you go. No court in the country would find you accountable for what happened."

He said nothing, just continued twirling the bottle.

"Do you blame yourself?"

"You ask a lot of questions," he muttered.

"I'm a lawyer. It's a requirement." She scooted around the edge of the tub so that she was sitting beside him and waited until he lifted his gaze to hers. "Jude, do you blame yourself?"

"Nah." He took another long pull from his beer. "I don't play that blame game. It happened. It sucked for everyone involved, especially for Seth. Nothing I can do to change it."

Uh-huh. That was a big, fat lie. "So you drink away your issues."

"No. I just don't look back. It's a philosophy that hasn't

done me wrong yet."

Now that lie she would call him on. "You're full of shit."

He said nothing more. Libby sighed and drank from her own bottle.

"So how is this bodyguard thing going to work?" she finally asked. "Are there rules or something?"

"We need to keep a low profile," he said, sounding more like his usual self. Back in his comfort zone. "I'll be in touch with my brothers, but otherwise, we'll have a strict no-contact policy. No phones, no Internet, no contact with anyone you know in D.C. Anyone around here asks, we're James and Liza Wilson."

"Who are they?"

"Us. Greer pulled some strings, got us some fake IDs. We're honeymooners from Virginia, but I don't plan on giving anyone the opportunity to ask about us. We're going to stay in this house unless we absolutely have to leave for some reason, like for groceries. No beach trips."

"Stuck in Key West and I can't even go to the beach." She laughed humorlessly. "Figures."

"Hey, I'm no happier about it than you. I'd give anything to be out there right now dancing my legs off to that music."

Libby tilted her head and listened. She hadn't noticed until he mentioned it, but now the distant, joyful beat made her want to dance herself. Her instinctive response was to apologize for his having to stay here with her, and that pissed her off.

"I don't need you." She waved a hand. "Go dance, have fun. I'm sure there are plenty of women out there, too. Easy pickings."

Jude sat up straighter and set his beer on the edge of

the tub. "You know, I don't particularly like this opinion you have of my sex life."

"And whose fault is that?"

"Libby, you can't keep holding the past against me or this is going to be a very long mission. I was young—"

"And stupid." She rolled her eyes, finished off her beer. "Save it. I was naive. So very naive to think a player like you would fall in love with a nerd like me."

"Goddammit, I did—" Jude half rose out of the tub, but caught himself and bit off whatever he'd been about to say. He sank back into his seat, swiped up his beer bottle, and drank the remaining contents on one breath. "Maybe I've changed."

"Doubt it."

"What do you want me to say?" he asked with a hint of defeat in his tone. "That I didn't sleep with anyone after you? That I didn't date? Of course I did. It's been eight years, and I'm not a monk. There were men after me, weren't there?"

She didn't want to tell him the truth and took a sip of her beer to stall.

His brows drew together, a crease forming between them. "Weren't there?"

Her throat tightened. "One night with a guy in law school."

Silence fell between them, filled with the hum of the hot tub's jets.

God, she shouldn't have told him that. Worse, she shouldn't be jealous of all his nameless, faceless lovers. But as ridiculous and illogical as it was, it hurt to think that he had enjoyed sex with other women when her one attempt after him had been a miserable failure. Dammit, she wanted the pleasure he'd so freely given other women.

Just once.

"You owe me." The declaration popped out without her consent, her mouth acting before her brain fully processed the thought. But what the hell? Despite the impulsiveness of the idea, it was a good one. She could work out all of her sexual frustration tonight, on her terms, before it bubbled over into something uncontrollable and dangerous. Maybe he wouldn't even be as good as she remembered, and then she could erase the past eight years and start fresh.

"You. Owe. Me," she repeated, enunciating each word.

His brows lifted. "I do?"

"Oh, yeah. You may not have been celibate, buddy, but I damn near was. It was supposed to have been just the two of us for the rest of our lives, but you took that from me. You robbed me of eight years of my sexual life. So you owe me one night."

His eyelids dropped to half-mast, and he looked at her through his lashes. "Just one?"

"Yes. That's all. I'm tired of pretending I'm not still attracted to you. Since we have to live together for the foreseeable future, I want to get it out of the way now."

"So logical." A slow grin spread across his face. "But, Libs, you've been doing it all wrong if you think one night will satisfy either of us."

"I haven't been doing it at all, and that's the problem." She held up a finger. "One night, Jude. Take it or leave it."

He stood, and steam rose off his chest. Weighed down by the water, his shorts hung so low on his hips that she could see the tip of his very erect penis. "Oh, I'm definitely taking it."

Chapter Six

Jude hesitated, hating the way she backed up with his every step closer. He knew he looked predatory, knew she wasn't anywhere near ready for him to unleash the full force of his desire. But, damn, he couldn't help himself. He hadn't planned on making any advances, despite the memory of losing himself in her, which had been replaying in his mind since seeing her again. Now here she was, offering one night, and maybe he was a complete jerk, but he didn't have the willpower to walk away from that. He followed her retreat, his blood running hotter than it had in years. He was tired of denying himself what he wanted, what his body and heart had claimed as his own years ago.

She backed away until she banged into the covered pool table. Which was perfect.

"Wait." She held up her hands, pushed against his chest as he crowded her, caging her in with a hand on each side of her hips.

"Second thoughts already?" He leaned in and scraped his teeth along the line of her chin to her ear. "Gotta tell me now."

"No. I don't know. Maybe we should think…" Her words trailed off into a moan as he traced the curve of her ear with his tongue, then tugged the lobe between his teeth.

"You think too much, Libs. Always have. Just feel."

She tilted her head to the side, allowing him better access, and he took that as consent. He grazed the column of her neck with his lips, enjoying the trail of goose bumps he left in his wake. Her hands found his hair, tangled in the longer strands on top, and guided his head down to a much more interesting area of the female anatomy. Happy to oblige, he sucked one of her nipples through the layers of her shirt and bra, but it wasn't enough. Too many damn clothes separated them. He needed her bare skin under his hand, against his tongue.

"You should have put your swimsuit on."

Resignation tinged her sigh. "I was afraid this would happen if I did."

"Hate to tell ya, babe, but this was gonna happen even if you were wearing chain mail." But, damn, he did like the thought of seeing her in a swimsuit. "That little purple bikini with the silver ties at the hips… You don't still have that, do you?"

Libby laughed and shook her head. "Of course not. I was twenty pounds lighter back then. It wouldn't fit me now."

"Mmm, I like your body now. All this soft skin here…" He stripped off her shirt and palmed her breasts. She'd always had the sexiest lingerie, and he was glad to see that hadn't changed, but right now he was more interested in the lovely mounds overflowing his palms and the rosy nipples straining toward him through the sheer white lace of her bra.

"And here…" In a move so quick it left her gasping, he spun her to face the pool table. He kissed her shoulder before dropping to his knees and sliding off her pants.

She groaned. "Jude—"

"No." His voice came out as little more than a rasp, and he stopped her from turning back around. Having her lace-covered ass right there in front of him was so damn erotic that the sight of her curves alone almost did him in. He traced a finger over the dimples at the base of her spine, lightly down the cleft between her cheeks, and found the honeyed spot between her legs already damp for him. Standing, he kept his hand on her sex and nudged her legs farther apart.

Christ, she was so wet. His cock ached with the need to sink into her, but he wasn't ready for that yet. He wanted to make her come, wanted her legs to turn to jelly, wanted her gasping and writhing and begging before he entered her. He slipped his fingers under the edge of her panties and enjoyed the shudder that shook her so hard she had to grab the pool table for support.

Oh yeah. She was wound so tight that he bet he could make her go off three times before he penetrated her.

This was going to be fun.

This was completely insane.

She'd promised herself she wasn't going to have sex with Jude ever again, had secretly nicknamed him "Last Man on Earth" Wilde—as in, not even if he were the last man on

Earth. Yet here she was, straining against his talented fingers, wanting nobody else.

A breeze stirred the palm fronds overhanging the pool and brushed her bare skin in a warm caress, reminding her they were still outside. She experienced a moment of sheer oh-my-God-I-must-have-lost-my-mind, but then Jude flipped aside the end of her ponytail and dragged his lips up her spine, gently biting the base of her neck as his fingers dipped deeper into her sex. Her knees threatened collapse. Only his muscled arm around her waist kept her from melting into a puddle of lust at his feet.

"We shouldn't be doing this," she squeaked.

"Yeah, we probably shouldn't." His breath was hot against her skin, and yet still sent goose bumps racing over her body. "But that's the fun of it."

Fun. Was this fun? As his lips and tongue continued their exploration of her spine and his fingers dipped in and out, in and out, she swallowed a moan. Oh, yes, this was fun. And delicious. And so very dangerous.

Crazy. This was all so crazy, and she didn't do crazy. She did safe. Secure. Steady.

Boring.

"You're thinking again," Jude said. He cupped her chin in one big hand and rubbed his thumb over her lower lip before drawing her toward him for a kiss that swept her up, shook her around, and spit her out in the land of impossible things.

She sucked in a sharp breath when he finally let her mouth go. "I'm not in Kansas anymore, am I?"

That devastatingly sexy grin of his spread across lips still damp from their kiss. "Nah, Dorothy, but this is no dream.

This is the real deal, and if you want to stop—well, damn, it might kill me, but I'll walk out that door right now and call one of my brothers to play bodyguard."

Her heart gave an unexpected lurch at the thought, which should have been all the proof she needed to back off and tell him to do exactly that. She'd probably be safer with one of his brothers, both physically and emotionally.

Instead, she found herself tracing his lips with her fingertip. Lips that so easily offered a smile. Lips that knew exactly how to make a woman scream with pleasure. Lips she had dreamed about more often than she wanted to admit even to herself. "If I say no, you won't stay?"

He shook his head. "Now that I've had a taste, I don't trust myself to be a gentleman and keep my hands off you."

"You've never been a gentleman, Jude Wilde."

"Exactly."

"Exactly," she echoed. Turning in the circle of his strong arms, she lifted herself up to sit on the pool table and wrapped her legs around his waist. If she was going to do this, she was throwing caution to the wind for one night and going all out. "So why start now?"

His answering grin was slow and sensuous. His hands were not as he wrestled her out of her panties and fumbled with her bra. She never remembered him fumbling before. He'd always been so sure of himself, so steady that it surprised her to see the tremble in his fingers. But then she had no interest in his fingers save for the deliciously wicked things they were doing between her legs again. He leaned in for a short kiss, sucked her lower lip into his mouth as he pulled away.

"Lay back," he whispered. "I want you in my mouth."

Her heart tripped, stuttered, and she was pretty sure she no longer knew how to breathe, but none of that mattered because he was staring at her like she was a feast and he was a man starved. She let him push her back, the padded, leather-like cover on the pool table cool against her bare skin. He gave a hum of male appreciation as his palm skimmed the front of her body, his gaze following until he found the soft curls at the vee of her legs. He slid two fingers into her again and shut his eyes, groaning as if in pain. She saw his hips pump almost involuntarily.

"You're still dressed," she managed between gasping breaths as his fingers continued their slide.

"For now." His voice was nothing but rasp, and the thrill of it made her muscles quiver. He was on the edge, just barely holding his desire in check. What she couldn't understand was, why? Jude Wilde never held back. Everything he did was in your face, in the moment, carpe diem. So why was he reigning himself in *now*?

"Jude." She waited until his lust-drunk gaze met hers, then deliberately opened her thighs, touched herself, and enjoyed the hitch in his breath while he watched. "You want your mouth on me? I'm waiting. Taste me."

His Adam's apple bobbed as he swallowed, and if that look in his eyes got any hotter, she'd be walking away from this with scorch marks. It would be worth it, though.

So worth it.

Jude dropped to his knees, hooked her legs over his shoulders and found her with his mouth. At the first lap of his tongue, she came in one hard spasm, thighs quaking, back arching, her cry echoing around the garden. And still he didn't stop, didn't let her ease back to Earth before he sent her into orbit again.

Definitely worth it.

In a burst of movement, as if he couldn't stand to be outside her a second longer, he surged to his feet, shed his shorts, dragged her to the edge of the table, and fisted himself in one hand, guiding his head to her entrance. With a hard thrust of his hips, he drove deep inside her.

"Wait," she managed even as she lifted to meet his thrusts. "Condom."

"I'm clean," he said between clenched teeth, pumped his hips again, and pleasure coiled tighter within her, curling her toes.

"I know. It's not that... Oh God, that feels so good." Her eyes nearly rolled back in her head, and she almost said to hell with it...but one thought stopped her. Pregnancy. She did not want a child with a man who acted like a child himself most of the time. She was lucky she hadn't ended up pregnant and alone eight years ago, and she wasn't going to take that risk this time around.

She smacked her hands against his chest. "Jude, wait. We need a condom. I'm not on birth control."

A stream of colorful curses fell from his lips, and she instantly regretted the lost connection when he left her and ran into the house. He was back a moment later and slapped a string of condoms—at least a half dozen—onto the pool table.

She laughed. "Now that's wishful thinking."

"You said one night, not one time. I plan to make the most of it." He ripped one open with his teeth, rolled it on, and found her again in one long glide. Slow, torturous thrusts and it wasn't enough. She didn't want slow and sweet from him. Didn't want gentle. She wanted sweaty, down-and-dirty, bed-rocking, flesh-slapping sex and wound her legs around his waist, lifted her hips, dug her heels into his back.

Spurred him on. Faster, harder.

He gave her exactly that until the sturdy pool table wobbled and creaked and sweat slicked both of them.

Tension wound so tightly inside Libby she thought she might pop like a container under too much pressure. She bit the inside of her cheek, determined not to cry out again. They were in the middle of a city, and although the stone fence and jungle-like garden blocked all views from the street, they did have neighbors. The whole block didn't need to know what they were up to tonight. But then Jude leaned forward, changing the direction of his thrusts as his lips closed over one beaded nipple and tugged.

And that was it.

The climax ripped a scream from her throat. After one more deep thrust, she felt him tighten up, felt his erection jump as he joined her, roaring with his own orgasm.

Jude collapsed but caught himself on his arms before crushing her. He stared at her for a long time as his breath sawed from his lungs, his gaze searching hers for...something. She didn't know what.

"Christ," he whispered. Finally shutting his eyes, he leaned his damp forehead against hers as shudders continued to wrack his body. "Oh, Christ. I can't get enough of you. I can't get enough."

He lurched upright, pulled off the condom, and grabbed another.

"No way. You can't possibly..." Shocked, she watched him roll the second condom into place over his straining erection. Even more shocking, she felt herself getting wet again, responding to his need, her sex tender but plumped and ready for him. "Jude, if we keep this up, I won't be able to walk tomorrow."

When he lifted his head and grinned at her with the devil in his eyes, she decided walking was overrated anyway. She reached for him, wrapped her hand around his length, and guided him to her. He caught her legs in one arm, hooked them over his shoulder, and drove into her like a man possessed, but she was right there with him, and she didn't last long.

This time, she didn't worry about the neighbors hearing.

Chapter Seven

She couldn't move. She was never going to be able to move again. And she was perfectly okay with that.

As the first rays of sunlight peaked through the trees and dappled the sex-rumpled sheets with dancing shadows, Jude lifted his head from the pillow where he had collapsed after the latest round of wall-pounding sex. His breathing still hadn't quite settled—for that matter, neither had hers—and his hair stuck up in charming bedhead spikes. Probably didn't help any that she had spent hours last night tugging at it, dragging her fingers through it. All that dark, rakishly long hair was soft as a kitten's coat, and she couldn't get enough of it. Even now, she had to fight the urge to run her fingers through the strands one more time.

Scowling, he squinted toward the wall of windows. "Shit," he muttered and stuffed his face back into the pillow, muffling another curse.

"What's wrong?"

"It's morning."

Libby watched the palms in the garden sway to a gentle morning breeze. Tried to tell herself that the bitter mix of emotion in the pit of her stomach wasn't disappointment. "Yes, it is."

"So it's over."

She rolled her lips together and made sure her voice was steady before speaking. "Yes. It's over."

"Unless…" He turned his head on the pillow. Brows raised over hopeful eyes the same color as the morning sky outside the window. "We make it a full twenty-four-hour deal?"

Tempting. But if she gave in, she'd always give in. She was well aware she had a weakness where Jude Wilde was concerned, and she couldn't let it get the better of her. Not again. Living through that heartbreak once in a lifetime was enough, thank you very much. "No. One night. That's all."

"That's what I thought." He sighed and pushed himself upright, swung his legs over the edge of the bed. "All right."

All right? That was all he had to say? Just…all right? She'd expected a protest, possibly a fight. At the very least, a complaint. Not this easy acceptance. He had to be plotting something devious. "What are you up to, Jude?"

"Right now, I'm going to shower. Unless you want it first?"

She shook her head.

"Okay. Shower, then I'm gonna eat something and crash for a couple hours. It was a long night." He spoke of it as if he'd spent the night at work, on a stakeout or whatever else he and his brothers did at that security office, rather than making love to her.

No, she corrected herself. Sex. There had been no love-making between them—nothing gentle or tender, and that was exactly what she'd wanted. So she had *no* reason to feel hurt about his blithe compliance with her wishes. None whatsoever. The burning sensation behind her eyelids was just from lack of sleep.

Jude stood and stretched his arms high over his head, his back arching, arms and shoulders flexing. God, he had a magnificent body. All sinewy muscle with just a faint dusting of dark hair in all the right spots. Highlighted by the sunshine, his body was a gilded work of masculine art that no straight woman in her right mind would be able to resist.

And that had always been the problem, hadn't it? No woman could resist him, and he used that power to his full advantage.

An intricate tribal tattoo followed the entire length of his spine and flared out into broken angel wings on his shoulders. A pair of dog tags hung from one wing, a pair of ballet slippers from the other, and on closer inspection, she realized it wasn't some abstract tribal design picked off the wall of a tattoo parlor. It had meaning, symbolized something important to him.

"Are all those swirls words?"

He glanced over his shoulder, confusion lining his forehead until he realized what she was referring to. "Yeah."

She squinted. Without her glasses, it was impossible to read from this distance, but when she tried to scoot across the bed to get a better look, he turned around.

"What does it say?" she asked.

"Nothing."

Okay. Sore subject. Even as curiosity niggled at her, she

promised herself she wouldn't ask about the tattoo again.

Jude crossed to his still-packed bag and unzipped it. "I know I said we had to share the bed, but I was just being an ass. You can have it. I don't mind the couch."

Another surprise. What was this, *Invasion of the Body Snatchers*? "Uh, okay. Thanks."

He found a pair of shorts and a shirt, tossed them both over one shoulder, and straightened. "What?"

"What?" she echoed.

"You're staring at me like you've never seen me before."

"Oh." Maybe because she was starting to get the feeling that she hadn't seen him before. Not really. She made herself look away, down—anywhere but at him—and realized she was still naked. She snatched the bedsheet up and hugged it to her breasts. "You just look different. Not like I remember."

"I'm older," he said.

"So am I. I have to ask, what's with the earring?"

"Got it last week to piss Reece off."

Now that was a typical Jude response. Maybe this was less pod person and more a bad case of the morning afters. Under normal circumstances, right now would probably be about the time he made his usual quick escape. Instead, he was stuck here with her, and his uncertainty about what to do next showed through the cracks in his charm, which had always been at its thinnest in the mornings.

As much as she enjoyed watching him squirm, she figured she should let him off the hook. "Go shower. I want to eat first anyway. I'm starving."

With a weak smile, he all but bolted into the bathroom. She waited until she heard the beat of the water spray against the shower walls before climbing out of bed and finding something to wear in her own bag.

If he wanted to act like she was just one more notch on his bedpost, fine. Because that was all he was to her—a notch, a good time, a lay.

Yup, she thought as she padded out to the kitchen. Jude Wilde meant nothing to her. Nothing at all.

Chapter Eight

Holy hell, she really *had* meant only one night.

Jude stared through the sliding patio doors at her in wonder. He'd thought for sure after the rocking good time they'd had, she was going to be supple, sexy putty in his hands for the rest of their stay in Key West. Maybe if he gave her enough pleasure in bed, she'd even consider giving him a chance to prove that he wasn't the kind of man she thought he was.

The kind of man he let her believe he was.

But there she sat, sunbathing in one of the loungers with the cat snoozing by her feet, completely ignoring him for a book. And it wasn't even the good kind, like one of the action-packed, edge-of-your-seat thrillers Camden often read. No, it was a history of criminal law in Revolutionary America.

Boring.

In fact, she'd had her nose buried in one dull book after

another all week. She'd barely said more than ten words to him since their first night here, and she definitely hadn't touched him again, which was starting to drive him a little bit insane. He needed to feel her hands on him. Her mouth. Needed to feel her tight body giving way to his invasion, over and over again until—

Jude cursed and paced away from the window. He was losing his fucking mind. As much as he loved this house, the walls were starting to close in on him, and the air felt thick in his lungs despite the blasting A/C. Her scent permeated everything, hanging in the air like a vanilla fog. He was suffocating, boredom and unquenched desire making for a smothering blanket. He had to get out. Had to do… something.

He glanced over his shoulder. Libby hadn't moved, hadn't acknowledged his presence in any way. She wouldn't miss him if he stepped out for a few, and with this place wired up like the freakin' Federal Reserve, he could set his phone to warn him at the slightest hint of trouble. He doubted there would be any. The twice-daily e-mails he got from his brothers said everything was mostly quiet on the home front. They had found the blue car that tried to run Libby down abandoned in a mall's parking lot, but it gave no clues as to the identity of her stalker. It had been stolen from an apartment building three miles from her office complex, and the owner was a pregnant woman on round-the-clock bed rest. She hadn't even known her car was missing until Camden showed up on her doorstep with the news.

Dead end.

Jude's brothers were monitoring K-Bar and his gang, as well as remotely monitoring Libby's home. So far, the gang hadn't even acknowledged in passing that they knew where she lived, nor had they so much as congratulated each other on scaring her off with the notes and dolls.

Something wasn't adding up, but it was up to his brothers to do the math. He was just the glorified babysitter, which was exactly why he had to get out of the house for a bit. Being cooped up was bad enough. Cooped up with a woman he wanted and couldn't touch?

Total. Hell.

Mind made up, he headed toward the front door. A walk on the beach. That's all he needed. He'd be gone twenty minutes, tops.

He'd never been one to sit still and relax. After his teachers had all but given up on him, the school shrink tried to convince his father that he needed medication. David Wilde had told the shrink to stuff those meds in a very uncomfortable place, and then dragged his ten-year-old son out of the school by the scruff of his neck. Jude had half expected punishment from his tough-as-nails, Army-bred father. Instead, he got a trip to the Smithsonian. David walked him through the museum, quizzing him ruthlessly on everything they saw. It had been an awesome day. Fun. Interesting. Nothing like sitting at a desk for hours at a time, reading out of a textbook.

Finally, his father stopped walking and muttered under his breath, "Those effing teachers aren't doing it right." With a grin, he looped an arm around Jude's shoulders. "Let's go get some burgers, huh?"

Christ. A surge of intense sadness made Jude's stomach hurt, and he stopped short halfway across the front porch. He hadn't thought about that day in years. Hadn't let himself because barely a week after that, his parents were gone, and it had been his fault. His carelessness, his reckless disregard for everyone around him, had gotten them killed.

He turned and studied the house's brightly painted siding, imagined red splattered over the white front door, imagined coming back from the beach and finding a naked paper doll pinned to it. Worse, not red paint, but blood. Libby's blood.

No. No way. Not happening on his watch.

Resigning himself to a fate of extreme boredom for the duration of this mission, he pulled open the door—

Libby tumbled into his arms. The light coconut scent of sunscreen filled his head as her bare skin, still warm from the sun, pressed to his. Her breasts flattened against his chest, and her arms wrapped around his neck, holding on tight.

Jude didn't know what he'd done to deserve this sudden show of affection, but man, did it ever feel good. He dipped his head, sought her mouth with his, and some of the tension coiled up in him eased.

This. This was what he needed, not a walk on the beach.

For a moment, she not only allowed the kiss, but participated, her tongue meeting and mingling with his. Her nipples stiffened under the fabric of her bathing suit top, poked into his chest with unyielding urgency. She rubbed against him like a cat seeking its master's hand, all needy and trying to be coy about it.

Well, he didn't do coy.

He hauled her into his arms and spun, slamming the front door shut and pinning her up against the wood. He pressed his pelvis to her belly, showing her exactly what he wanted and how much he wanted it. She moaned deep in her throat and dug her fingers into his shoulders. Without breaking away from her mouth, he gripped her lovely ass in both hands and lifted her, pumping against her in a panto-mime of sex. Her legs circled his waist, and she arched into each thrust, so ready he could feel the wetness of her desire through the layers of clothes separating them.

Too many layers. Fuck, he needed her naked, needed to pound into her until her orgasm locked her body around him and tore his own release from his cock.

Jude reached around and tugged on the knot of her bikini, but the movement was too fast, too insistent, and she froze in his arms.

Goddammit, she couldn't keeping doing this to him, run-ning so damn hot that her lust was all but combustible in one instant and then giving him the cold shoulder the next. He tightened his grip around her and stilled his hips. He tasted her again, softening the kiss, trying to tell her in action what he'd never be able to explain in words. She melted into him, and for a second, he thought he'd won this battle.

She bit down on his lower lip. Hard.

"Ow!" He jerked backward. "Son of a bitch!"

"What do you think you're doing?" she demanded and shoved his shoulder. "Put me down."

He did. His lip felt numb. He ran his tongue over it to make sure he wasn't bleeding. Nope, no blood but he needed a cold compress or else he was going to end up with a swollen lip. "What was that for?"

"I told you—one night. Just one. We did it. It was fun. It's *not* happening again."

"Why the hell not? And, hold up a second. *You* hugged *me*. Your legs wrapped around my waist."

She slapped his chest. "I tripped, you idiot. You startled

me when you yanked open the door, and I reacted…badly. Where were you going anyway?"

"Nowhere."

Crossing her arms over her chest, she gave him a look that clearly said *yeah, right.* "You were in an awful big hurry for going nowhere. Were you leaving?"

"I needed some air." As if that excuse wasn't transparent as fuck. Annoyed with himself, the situation—every-damn-thing—he stalked past her, intending to grab a beer from the kitchen.

She caught his arm. "Dad won't be happy about you trying to leave when he's paying you to guard me."

He ground his teeth. "He's not here, and you can't contact him so, tell me, how's he going to find out if I go for a walk?"

"Jesus. You have got to be the worst bodyguard in the history of the profession."

"I never claimed to be good at this. Hell, I never wanted this job in the first place. Greer forced me into it, told me I had to face my mistakes or some shit. Well, fuck that. There's a reason I never look back—and you're it. I never wanted to see you again. You drive me nuts with all of your questions and protests and fucking logic. You're so uptight, you wouldn't know a good time if it whacked you on the ass."

Libby flinched and dropped her hand from his arm. He thought he should feel like an asshole, and probably would later after he cooled off, but right now, his anger ran too hot.

Apparently, so did Libby's, because after her initial shock wore off, she struck back. "You think you're so great to live with? At least I act my age. You're like a spoiled child. You can't sit still for more than a minute, and you mope around here like you lost your puppy! Life's not all fun and games. Seriously, Jude, grow the hell up."

Grow up? He glowered at her back as she turned on her heel and marched away with her chin held high. First Reece, and now her. Christ, he was fucking sick of people telling him that. So he liked to cut loose, have fun. Did it really make him such a horrible person because he lived it up every chance he got?

No. He didn't think so. He worked hard when work beckoned. He just played harder. Nothing wrong with that.

If anything, Libby was in the wrong here. Too uptight, too practical, too logical. Outside the bedroom, she had no concept of fun as far as he could tell, which was a damn shame because the girl he remembered knew how to have good time whenever, wherever, and however she could. She'd been shy, but adventurous and vivacious once he knocked down all of her self-containing walls, and he couldn't assimilate the Libby of today with the Libby of yesterday. They were two completely different people.

And he'd made her this way.

Every ounce of irritation in Jude drained away at that sobering thought. He'd lost his shit after their split, diving headlong into his burn all bridges and take no prisoners approach to life, but Libby must have done the opposite, withdrawing further into herself and throwing all of her energy into earning her law degree.

Damn. He'd destroyed her confidence, smothered that spark he'd once found so attractive. At this point, any kind of forgiveness or reconciliation was a pipe dream, but he could give her some of her old self back. It'd be a helluva challenge, but she deserved it.

He drifted toward the patio doors and peeked outside. She'd gone back to her book in one of the loungers by the pool.

Perfect.

Backing up, he edged out the front door and stopped on the porch to scan the garden. Didn't take long to find what he was looking for: a large, deep pink bloom that all but sparkled with life and color—exactly like the Libby he remembered. He leaned over the railing and plucked it from its plant, tested its scent. Sweet, also like Libby.

Yes, he thought, twirling the stem between his fingers as he walked back into the house. This definitely might take a while.

Good thing he had nothing but time on his hands.

Chapter Nine

Libby heard a splash and lowered her book. It was too small of a sound to have been Jude jumping in for a swim, and a sharp spike of worry made her set her book aside.

"Sam?"

Not that Sam would voluntarily go anywhere near the water's edge. In typical feline fashion, he hated being wet, but there was always a chance he could've fallen in...

Nope, he still lay curled up at her feet, dozing contentedly in the sun. He lifted his head at the sound of his name and blinked his big green eyes as if to say, "Yes?"

She scratched under his chin. "Nothing, kitty cat. Go back to sleep."

So what had made the splash? She scanned the pool's surface and saw nothing. Okay, maybe she imagined it. It was more than possible. She'd been so absorbed in her book that she didn't even realize how late it was getting. The sun had been high in the sky when she came out here to get away from Jude, but now slanted across the patio at a stark angle, casting shadows over the pool.

She really should go inside and face Jude. Couldn't avoid him forever. Besides, she was getting hungry.

With a sigh, she crawled off the lounger and stretched her arms up over her head. Her body felt loose and warm from the sun, her muscles more relaxed than they had been in years, but she still couldn't shake the notion that she was shirking her responsibilities by taking time off from work. Yes, it was time she'd earned. And, yes, other people took time off with no repercussions. It didn't make her less of a lawyer, somehow inferior to her counterparts.

And still.

Maybe she could sneak some work in tomorrow. Jude usually swam laps for an hour or so in the morning. She could do it without him knowing. A quick call to Noah for an update, a couple e-mails... Really, what would it hurt? She highly doubted K-Bar had the kind of technology needed to track her all the way down to Florida from one little phone call to her office.

The idea of work cheered her as she turned around to gather her things—and spotted a huge green monster swimming across the pool toward her.

She shrieked and dropped both her book and towel. The book skidded across the concrete deck and landed in the water with a soft plop. The towel disappeared from view, but she didn't dare drop her gaze to look for it. Not with that... thing...swimming closer. Closer. Closer.

Sam hissed and arched up onto his toes, and she snatched him up in a hug, unmindful of his extended claws.

Closer. Closer.

She couldn't move, her knees locked in terror. She imagined giant teeth clamping on to her leg, pulling her under the surface until water filled her lungs and choked her. Powerful jaws ripping through muscle and bone and dragging her dead body away. Nobody would know what happened to her until the alligator died and someone cut it open and found what was left of her in its belly.

Oh God.

"Libby!" Jude appeared in the patio doorway in nothing but his boxer-briefs, his hair mussed from a recent nap. He held his gun in a two-handed grip in front of him, but kept it pointed toward the ground as he edged to her side. He ran a hand over her hair, her arms, and her back as if checking for injuries, then took the terrified cat out of her arms and set him on the ground. Sam tore off toward the house in a streak of orange fur, and Jude returned his full attention to her. He clasped her neck, made her look at him with the pressure of his thumb against her jaw.

"What's wrong? Hey, Libs, talk to me. Are you okay? What did you see?"

Unable to force sound through her frozen vocal cords, she pointed a shaking finger at the pool. He turned…and laughed.

Laughed. At an *alligator.*

He really was crazy.

"Is that all?" He set his gun on the table between loungers and knelt at the edge of the pool. In a move so fast all she could do was squeak in protest, he snatched the thing out of the water by its tail and the back of its spiked neck. It opened its mouth, but instead of rows of deadly teeth, it had nothing but pink gums and a darting lizard tongue.

Libby scrambled backward over the lounger as Jude turned toward her with the reptile in hand. "W-what the hell is that?"

"Iguana," he said and loosened his grip on its neck. The iguana bumped its head against his hand, and he smiled. "A friendly one, too. He just wanted to say hi. Maybe bum some fruit off you. C'mere and pet him."

"I don't think so." She stumbled back another step, her heart still hammering painfully. "W-where did it come from?"

"They're all over around here. People let their pets go when they got too big to care for, and they started breeding in the wild. They like to snack on garden flowers, which is probably why this guy found his way here. Just looking for an evening snack, huh, buddy?"

He spoke as if he planned to let it stay in the garden. He would probably tease her relentlessly, but she couldn't deal with that. Just…couldn't. Sure, it wasn't an alligator like she first thought, but it was huge and looked like a prehistoric throwback from her worst reptile-themed nightmare.

"It's okay," Jude said and took another step forward. "He's harmless."

"Please—" She choked on a surge of fear-induced tears. "Please, don't. Can you…get rid of it?"

Jude stopped. Frowned. "He scares you."

"Yes. Very much." *And here comes the teasing*, she thought. If he did something childish like throw it at her or chase her around the pool with it, she was going to murder him. Slowly. In his sleep. After chopping off his balls.

"Oh, damn." He backed away from her in three quick

steps. "I'm sorry. I didn't realize… I'm an idiot. Let me get him outta here. I'll take him down to the beach where there's plenty of tourists to feed him so he won't be tempted to come back." As he spoke, he circled around the other side of the pool and headed for the path to the back gate. "Go inside and lock the doors. I'll be right back."

As her wobbly knees finally gave out, Libby sank onto one of the loungers and stared after him in complete shock. Why hadn't he teased her? She'd given him plenty of ammunition between mistaking the iguana for an alligator and squealing like a terrified child when he tried to get her to pet it. The Jude she knew wouldn't have let it go. The heartless bastard would have been relentless about it, too, teasing her until she was sobbing…

But he hadn't.

In fact, he'd looked horrified that he'd unintentionally frightened her. He'd even walked the long way around the pool so that the damn lizard wouldn't be anywhere near her. That was…thoughtful. And kind of…well, surprisingly sweet.

"Who are you?" she whispered into the gathering dusk. Because whoever this man was, he definitely was not the Jude Wilde she once knew.

Jude dropped the iguana on a rock wall by the beach, much to the delight of the tourists watching the sun's fiery decent over the ocean. It was only then, as dozens of cameras turned his way, that he realized he was still dressed for a nap—in nothing but his underwear. His only concern had been getting Mr. Iguana as far away from Libby as possible to erase that terrified expression from her face, and he hadn't given his state of dress—or, rather, undress—a second thought.

But, hell with it. It was Key West. He'd seen stranger things than a man running around in boxer-briefs, carrying a lizard.

Wary of leaving Libby for too long, he gave the crowd a wave, then beat feet the block and a half back to the house. He found her exactly where he'd left her, sitting on the end of the lounger.

"Libby, I told you to go inside."

Her eyes looked huge in the gathering darkness, and even a dolt like him could see the glaze of shock in them. He cursed himself yet again and knelt beside her. "I'm sorry I frightened you."

"No, it wasn't—" She lifted a shaking hand to her temple and let go a humorless laugh. "I thought it was an alligator."

"Crocodile," he corrected. "Alligators like fresh water. American Crocodiles live in salt water, but they're endangered, and you don't see them much this far south…" At her furrowed brow, he trailed off. "And that doesn't matter. I'm rambling. Sorry."

She tilted her head to one side and studied him with a curious expression. "You've been apologizing a lot lately."

"Yeah, well. I got a lot to apologize for, don't I?" Heat crawled across the back of his neck, and he hoped like hell he wasn't turning red. To cover, he gripped her by the wrists and lifted her to her feet. "How about we go inside now? Get some coffee and I'll put in a movie."

Some of the color returned to her complexion as he led

her toward the house. "If you put in *Lake Placid*, I swear I'll make you into a soprano."

"Aw, give me some credit, Libs. I have a more refined pallet than that when it comes to movies." He settled her on the couch and then backed up a couple steps before adding with a grin, "I was thinking *Godzilla.*"

"I will slaughter you," she said and wrapped herself up in the thin quilt from the back of the couch, but the threat lacked heat, and a smile played around her lips. It pleased him that she'd bounced back enough from the scare to start issuing threats.

"All right, no giant reptiles." He opened the cabinets in the entertainment center and found a dismal selection of highbrow dramas and lowbrow comedies. Apparently, Seth's tastes in movies hadn't changed. "We'll order something On Demand."

"That bad?" Libby asked.

He winced. "Painful."

As he straightened, Libby cleared her throat. "Um, Jude, you do know you're still in your underwear, right?"

"I'm aware."

"And that you ran out in public like that?"

"Eh." He waved a hand, but decided that maybe it was time to pull on some shorts. "Key West is like Vegas. What happens here, stays here. I'll get dressed, maybe pop us some corn." He handed her the remote, and the quilt fell away as she reached for it. Angry red lines marred the soft flesh of her arm.

"What the hell?" Forgetting about everything else, he caught her wrist and turned her arm over when she tried to hide the marks. "That fucking cat."

"Don't be mad at him." She tugged, trying to loosen his grip. "It wasn't his fault."

"Bullshit. He scratched the hell out of you." Jude ran his fingers gently over the scratches, then dropped her wrist and changed course for the small bathroom off the living room. He tore open cupboards, looking for the first-aid kit that Seth kept there. It had seen a lot of use during their partying days, always kept well stocked with everything from antiseptic cream to sutures to IV bags and tubing. He found it and started back across the living room. "I need to clean you up."

"Why?"

"Because that cat shits in a box and then digs through it. I can't even begin to guess the kinds of bacteria he carries around on his paws."

"Not that. I agree that I need to clean these scratches, but...why do you care?"

Her words hit him with the force of a surface-to-air missile, and he stopped short halfway across the living room. Why did he care? The question implied awe and disbelief, as if he were doing something so far out of the realm of her understanding she couldn't wrap her mind around it. And, damn, that hurt, because he'd never stopped caring. For him, it was a fact of life—inevitable, like the spin of the Earth on its axis. No matter what he did, thought, or pretended, Elizabeth Pruitt was always going to mean something to him.

Not like he could tell her that. No, he'd had his reasons for ending things with her the way he had—reasons that still applied. So instead of saying any of the thoughts on his mind, he answered, "It's my job. Your father hired Wilde Security to keep you safe from everything, including cats."

She frowned. "Sam was just scared."

"Scared or not, all cats are insane," he said and settled onto the couch next to her. He set the first-aid kit on the coffee table, flipped it open, and searched for the antiseptic pads.

"Wait, let me get this straight." She held up her hands to stop him from dabbing any of the scratches. "You like freaky giant lizards, but not cats?"

"Yeah, pretty much. Cats always look like they're plotting your demise."

"And the lizard wasn't?"

"Nah. He just wanted to steal a flower or two." He caught her wrist and slapped one of the pads over the scratches.

She hissed through her teeth. "*You* are the only insane one in this room."

"So you've said. Repeatedly. Now hold still. It doesn't hurt."

She grumbled, but let him finish tending to her arm. After a long moment, she muttered, "You're kind of good at this."

"I had some battlefield medical training."

"All so you could tend to cat scratches."

"Yeah, well." With a shrug, he packed up the kit and started gathering the used bandage wrappers. "I'd much rather be here, dealing with cat scratches, than over there, dealing with a buddy's bullet wound."

"God. That was so insensitive of me. I apologize. I'm still shaken, I guess." She hesitated, swallowed hard. "Did you ever see one? A bullet wound?"

"And worse."

She bit her lower lip. "Were you…?"

"No, I never took a bullet."

"But you were shot at?"

"Few times. Lucky for me, we had better snipers. Seth saved my ass more times than I want to admit." He picked up the kit, the wad of wrappers, and used antiseptic pads. "Figure out what movie you want to watch. I'll be back in a few."

Without giving her time to respond, he returned the kit to its spot in the bathroom, then strode to the bedroom. Once inside, he leaned against the cool wood. Drew in several deep breaths.

Smile, he told himself. Just smile.

Damn, she had a way of picking at him until he felt things he didn't want to feel. Things he tried so very hard to block from his memory. Things like the feel of a buddy's blood seeping onto his hands from mortal wounds, the fear that he'd never make it home in once piece, the knowledge that if he did, he was going back to an empty house because he'd ruined the one good thing he'd ever had...

The past was the past, he reminded himself. No sense in dwelling on things that he couldn't change. Bridges burned for a reason...and blah blah blah.

Dragging his hands through his hair, he shoved away from the door and grabbed his basketball shorts from the floor. As he yanked them on, he made himself smile.

But part of him in the deepest, darkest pit in his soul wondered how long he could keep smiling.

Chapter Ten

A spatter of color against the kitchen counter caught Libby's attention as she came inside from the pool the following morning, and she finally pulled her nose out of the book she'd found tucked away on the shelf in the living room. The light and fluffy romance wasn't her usual reading preference, but since her other book had taken a swim during the lizard fiasco, she'd picked this one up out of desperation—and she hadn't been able to put it down. The hero was just too…yummy. Not the perfect man, by any means, but close enough that she kind of wished he was real. She hadn't realized how much time had passed since she started reading until the sun's rays became brutal and she had to go inside or risk sunburn. Even so, she planned to get a glass of ice tea, curl up somewhere quiet, and finish the book.

Except that flash of color was out of place on the dark granite counter top and Libby backtracked to get a better look.

A flower.

Surprised, she lifted it to her nose and scanned the house's open floor plan for Jude. Why would he pick a flower? And then just leave it sitting here without water? Here, where she'd be sure to see it…

She scowled at the book, which she'd laid on the counter when she picked up the flower. Its candy-colored cover showed a shirtless man in a pair of low-riding jeans, his very fine backside turned to the reader, with a rose in his hand, hidden behind his back for the unsuspecting heroine. The hero had spent most of the book trying to seduce his love with flowers, which made him charming.

Not so much with Jude, who had hinted oh so casually this morning that Seth's sister was a book addict and since this used to be the Harlan family's vacation house before Seth moved in fulltime, Abby may have left something behind for her to read.

That conniving…sweet…no, definitely conniving jerk!

Incensed, she stepped on the trash can pedal to open the lid and dropped the perky pink flower in. She started to toss the book in after it, but hesitated. She knew the hero would get his woman in the end, and yet, she had to finish reading it. She could use a happily ever after in her life right now, so she let the lid drop and set the book aside on the counter. She'd come back to it later. Right now, she had to set a certain thick-skulled man straight about their relationship. Again.

She thought he was in the garage, so she started when she marched into the living room and found him sprawled facedown on the couch, sound asleep. Should've figured as much—he was an early riser and afternoon-nap taker, after all. One arm hung limply off the side of the cushion, and his bare feet stuck out over the couch's arm. His T-shirt had ridden up in his sleep, showing a glimpse of his deeply tanned skin and the ink of that back tattoo he was so protective of. Curiosity overrode her annoyance, and she drifted closer.

What was that tattoo? It wasn't "nothing" like he'd said. It meant something to him, and she couldn't help it, she was dying to find out what. The dog tags, the ballet slippers, the intricate swirls of words… What did it all signify?

Sam lay on the far arm of the couch by Jude's head, curled up, his green eyes focused with unblinking intent on Jude. Maybe the cat was plotting his demise after all. The two got along about as well as cops and criminals. Still, she was inexplicably pleased to see them sharing the same piece of furniture without incident.

If Jude didn't notice Sam on the couch with him, he must be sound asleep. So maybe she could sneak up, take a better look at that tattoo of his…

Just a quick peek. He'd never even know.

On quick, silent feet, she tiptoed around to the other side of the couch and leaned over the back. No movement from him, not even a finger twitch. Oh, yeah, she could march the entire beach crowd through the living room right now, and he wouldn't have the slightest idea.

Out. Cold.

She tugged lightly at the hem of his T-shirt, exposing another inch of bronzed skin, then another—

And before she drew her next breath, he grabbed her, flipped her over the back of the couch and had her pinned under him. She squeaked in alarm, and as the fog of sleep cleared from his eyes, he loosened his grip.

"What were you doing?" he demanded, sleep still coating his voice in rust.

"I was only checking to see if you were awake."

"By stripping me?" He yawned and rubbed his free hand over his face. "Huh. Interesting way to wake a guy. I feel kinda violated."

"Liar." Flustered, she struggled against his hold. The twinkle in his no-longer-sleepy eyes proved he was enjoying this too much. Great. What a way to give him more ammunition. "Let me up."

He pretended to think about it for all of a half second. "Nuh-uh. I like you under me." His hips pressed into hers, and the bulge of his erection prodded her through her skirt, hit just the right spot. She had to bite the inside of her cheek to keep from moaning, but her body still betrayed her, arching up to meet his.

A smile inched up one side of his lips. "*You* like you under me."

With his hand still on her neck, his thumb stroking back and forth over her pulse point, there was no way he couldn't feel the way her blood pressure spiked at his words.

"You know I do, dammit. But I told you—"

"One night. Yeah." He grumbled something under his breath, but finally rolled off her and gained his feet. Hands resting on his lean hips, his body still very aroused, he stared down at her. "You are the most frustrating woman I know."

"Wow. That's saying something, since you've known scores of them."

His jaw clenched together so hard she heard his back teeth grind. Without another word, he snapped up his phone from the end table and walked away.

Dammit. Libby sighed at herself and straightened, running her fingers through her tangled hair. Through the window, she watched him sit down on one of the loungers by the pool and check the screen of his phone. She'd only meant to aggravate him. His numerous sexual conquests bothered her, so of course, she had to keep picking away at them like a child picks at a scab.

What she couldn't understand is why her mentioning his love life always seemed to hurt *his* feelings, too.

Three missed calls from Reece. And one from GQ, Colonel Pruitt's uppity lawyer.

Jude blew out a breath. Just what he didn't want to deal with right now when he had a raging case of blue balls and the only woman he wanted thought he was nothing more than man-whore.

He stole a glance inside the house, but Libby had left the living room and was nowhere to be seen.

Something had to give there. He didn't know what, but they couldn't keep going on like they had been.

He should talk to her. Talking had never had been something he was particularly good at or fond of—at least not when it came to the serious kind of talking that started or ended relationships, the kind that got messy with all sorts of emotion.

And speaking of messy…

He stared down at his phone, then hit the speed dial before he could talk himself out of it. If he didn't return those three calls, Reece would just blow up his phone until he answered. Then things would *really* get messy.

Reece didn't waste time with a greeting. "In. Your. Underwear. Really? I mean…*really*?"

Of all the things he'd expected this convo to be about, underwear hadn't been anywhere on that list. "What are you talking about?"

"Don't tell me you don't know," Reece all but growled. "You. On the beach. In your underwear. With a lizard. What fucking part of low fucking profile don't you get, Jude? I mean, fuck, you're a meme. You're all over the Internet."

The back of his neck heated. "*All* over?"

"Some tourist posted you on YouTube, and it went viral."

Jude gave himself a moment, just a moment, to wallow in the embarrassment, the shame, but then he gulped it all down and forced himself to laugh. "So I'm like an underwear model now. Maybe I'll get a commercial deal with Hanes."

"Jesus," Reece said, his tone one of complete awe. "You don't get it. You really don't. Goddammit, Jude, Pruitt and his fucking lawyer are both riding our asses, and we're pulling all-nighters up here. There's a woman and her family counting on you to keep her safe. A woman you supposedly cared about at one time, and you're running around like drunken frat boy, posing for tourists? Are you really that selfish and—" He broke off, sighed. "No, I'm done yelling. I can't deal with you anymore. I'm…done."

Jude's heart lodged in his throat, and speech was nearly impossible around it. "Reece—"

"Greer or one of the twins will be calling so keep the phone nearby. We need to make plans to get Libby out of there."

Oh shit. They couldn't take Libby out of here. It was

the safest place for her. "No! No, you're right, I screwed up again. Okay? But listen, the only people who know Libby is here with me are you guys, Seth, and Libby's father. The lawyer doesn't even know where we are, does he?"

"No," Reece said as if he had to unlock his jaw to get the sound out.

"And nobody else knows about our connection, so why would they suspect she's down here partying it up with me?"

Silence. He took that as acknowledgment he had a point, since Reece would never say so. "We're still okay. Our cover's intact, and unless you have another house somewhere just as secure, this is still the best place for her."

More silence. Then, grudgingly, "All right. First hint of trouble, we're pulling you both out."

"Understood."

Dead air. Jude winced and lowered the phone. He didn't know why it still hurt; Reece *never* said good-bye.

Figures. Even when he tried to be helpful, he managed to fuck things up.

He stood and returned to the house, feeling like he should keep Libby in his sights at all times now. Just in case. He believed what he told Reece—nobody should be able to make the connection between them, and this fortress of a house was the best place for her.

Still…

He didn't make it past the kitchen. The flower he'd left for Libby on the counter was gone. He spent a moment searching the floor, the sink, anywhere it could have dropped. Then he spotted the trash can against the wall, its lid open.

No. She didn't.

He tossed his phone on the counter and crossed to the

trash. On top of everything lay the flower. He had to pick a new one this morning, since the bloom from yesterday had wilted before Libby saw it, but this one was starting to wilt, too, and looked sad and pathetic on its bed of crumpled paper towels. He plucked it out with two fingers. Talk about kicking a guy when he was down. He started to toss it away again but stopped short and scowled at his refection in the patio doors.

Was he really just going to give up? Libby had spurned his advances nine years ago when he first saw her having lunch at that restaurant in Quantico with her father. If he'd given up back then... Well, they wouldn't be in the awkward position they were in now, with broken hearts and wounded prides. But there had been so many good times before the bad, and he wouldn't trade those precious memories for anything.

So, no, he decided and placed the flower on top of the trash can, accepting her challenge. Forget that crap defeatist attitude. He'd just have to keep trying.

Chapter Eleven

Another flower.

This time, he'd stuck it in the fridge. *Getting more creative*, Libby thought with a half laugh. Now he was making her seek them out like an Easter egg hunt. Every night she told herself she wouldn't play along again, and yet every morning, she couldn't help but peek into cupboards and other hidey-holes…discreetly, of course. At least until he went out for his swim. Then she turned the house upside down, searching. No way would she let him know that she actively sought out the flowers or that a little thrill went through her every time she found one.

Today's pick was a beautiful bluish-purple, the blossom as big as her fist. She pulled it out of the fridge and underneath it…

"Oh my God."

Her book! The one she'd dropped in the pool when the iguana paid them that unwelcome visit. Here it sat between the milk and a pitcher of ice tea, a brand new copy, the dust jacket all shiny and clean. Where had he gotten it? He hadn't left the house…except for the three times he ran out to the front gate and impatiently checked the mail yesterday.

Sneaky man.

She picked up the book, let the fridge door fall shut, and ran her fingers over the cover. This, she hadn't expected from him. He wasn't an insightful or thoughtful man. How had he known that once the burn of embarrassment and fear over the iguana ordeal wore off, she most regretted the loss of her book?

Libby set the book aside and turned her attention to the flower. It was so hard to stay annoyed at him when he pulled stunts like this. Twirling the stem between her fingers, she drifted over to the floor-to-ceiling windows overlooking the garden and tried to spot the plant it had come from. She had to give him credit for his stubborn perseverance. Any other man would have given up on this game by now.

After one last indulgent sniff of its petals, she smiled and tossed the flower in the trash. But the book…that she would keep. No sense in letting a good book go to waste, even if it was to prove her point.

Although, to be honest, she couldn't quite remember what exactly her initial point had been.

Jude watched through the window as Libby searched for and found his gifts in the fridge. She picked up the flower and buried her nose in its fragrant petals. For a second, just a sliver of time as she stood there, highlighted by a sunbeam with the flower in her hand and a secret smile curving her lips, hope had buzzed through his head and quickened his pulse.

Maybe this time…

But, no. She turned away from the window, stepped on the pedal of the trash can to open the lid, and tossed the flower just like all the others.

"Fuck." Jude shook his head and let himself have a moment to sulk. She had to be the most unromantically inclined woman ever. What was it going to take to get by all of her defenses?

But then he noticed her pick up the book he'd asked Camden to buy and overnight to him with Seth's name on the box. He'd had a helluva time talking his brother into it, but the way she hugged that book to her chest made it worth the fight. Hot damn. She was finally keeping something he'd given her. Why that made him want to dance, he didn't know, but he indulged in the urge and executed a tap-tap-slide around the pool that would have had his mother beaming with pride.

"Nice moves, Slick."

He spun and grinned at Libby. "Yeah?"

She smiled as she walked out onto the patio. "Seriously, I'm impressed. You can really dance. I never knew that about you."

"Yeah, well, Mom was a dance instructor." Two swaying steps put him close enough to snatch her into his arms and swing her around to the faint strings of guitar music coming from the beach a block away. "She made all five of us take lessons, always said a real man knew his way around a dance floor."

"And you *lived* through high school?"

"Yeah. I even made it cool."

"You would."

"Hey, it was a great way to pick up chicks."

She smacked his chest, but even that didn't dampen his mood. He spun her, dipped her. When she straightened, her hair fell out of its clip and into her eyes.

She was laughing. "You are in a scary good mood all of a sudden."

By tacit agreement, neither of them ever mentioned the flowers, so he just grinned and spun her again. "I'd love to take you dancing for real sometime. We're good together in bed—no, don't get all huffy. Just stating a fact. We're good in bed, so we'd be dynamite on a dance floor."

"If I didn't have two left feet."

"Nah, that's not true."

She gave a disbelieving laugh. "I practically killed myself and everyone within five feet of me the one and only time I ever tried Zumba."

"You're just underpracticed." With one hand on the small of her back, he drew her into him until their bodies touched from chest to thigh. Swayed with her. She was inflexible as a rod at first, tense but not fighting him. He took that as a good sign and did the relaxing for her, closing his eyes and letting the soft chords of the guitar sink into his bones until the music guided his movements.

Slowly, ever so slowly, she loosened up, and her hips joined the rhythm of his. She melted into him, her arms around his waist, her head resting on his chest…and they fit. Just like his parents had when they used to dance across the kitchen, each body instinctively recognizing its missing half in the other.

Christ, why hadn't he noticed it before? Why hadn't she? It was so obvious.

The music stopped, but he didn't let go. There would be more soon. There was always music in Key West.

But at the sudden silence, she lifted her head from his chest. Dazed brown eyes blinked up at him, and every ounce of tension that had drained out of her poured back in—he felt her spine tense under his hand.

He tightened his grip and drew her tighter against him, lowered his head and found her mouth. His ever-present lust for her tried to turn the kiss into something hard and hungry, but that wasn't what she needed right now. Anything too rough or demanding would make her balk, so he consciously worked to soften his mouth. He kissed her with a dreamy intimacy, trying to show her with his lips all the things that he'd ever felt when it came to her but could never voice.

She wound her arms around his waist and kissed him back, her mouth soft and sweet until she changed the angle and took over. She plundered and claimed, curling her fingers into his hair, branding him with the intensity of her sudden, flaring need. Blood pounded from his brain into his cock, and he lost all sense of himself. He was Libby's man, and his only purpose in life was to give her pleasure.

Right. Now.

Panting, she broke away from the kiss. "Oh shit."

No, not yet. This perfect moment couldn't end yet.

Jude sucked in a breath and lowered his head again, intent on finding her mouth with his and reminding her of exactly how good they were together. How right.

She turned away, gave him her cheek instead of her soft

lips, then pushed against his chest when he drew back.

Yup, the moment was over.

After an internal struggle of epic proportions, he let her go and dropped his arms to his sides.

"Libby." He couldn't think of anything else to say, couldn't find the words.

She backed away so fast he was surprised she didn't trip over anything. "I'm going to make lunch," she said in a breezy tone, the subtext of which clearly stated that the last few minutes were *off limits* as far as conversation went. Before he managed a reply, she all but sprinted into the house.

Hell no. She wasn't going to pretend nothing happened. He wouldn't let her get away with it, not when he felt like his world had been rocked to its foundation. Whether she liked it or not, they fit together.

Jude dipped a hand in his pocket to rub the ever-present ring. Yeah, they *fit*. And she'd kept the book.

Chapter Twelve

"I told you, Noah. I'm not supposed to talk about it. For my own safety."

Jude stopped short as he stepped into the house from the patio with a towel raised halfway to his dripping hair. He'd been feeling pretty damn good this morning after his swim, had worked out the tension that kept winding tighter in him as each day passed. But as soon as he heard Libby's oh-so-practical voice chatting away in the living room, every knot returned to the exercise-loosened muscles of his back and shoulders.

Noah? As in Matchstick, her skinny, flame-haired assistant? Son of a bitch. She couldn't possibly be stupid enough to call him.

"I wish I could," she continued with resignation tingeing her voice, "but I have a Neanderthal of a bodyguard and— yes, that's the one. I know. I'm not particularly fond of him, myself, but you can rest easy. He's not going to stop me from working."

Cursing, Jude threw aside the towel and stalked across the kitchen, leaving wet footprints on the tile behind him. He found her seated at the computer desk in the office off the living room. As she started speaking legalese into the cell phone clamped to her ear, she clicked her way through a pdf file on screen.

"Are you fucking kidding me?"

She jumped and spun around in her seat.

"Are you fucking kidding me?" he repeated through his teeth and snatched the phone out of her hand. At the other end of the line, he heard Noah squawking with outrage, but ignored it and powered down the iPhone. He pulled it out of its protective case, strode to the patio doors, and fast-balled it into the pool before returning to the living room. He handed the case back and Libby stared down at it, shock widening her eyes behind her glasses.

"Jude, you son of a—"

He held up a finger to silence her. "No phones. I thought I made that clear."

"Bullshit. You said no such thing."

"I told you our first night here. No phones. No computer. No contact with anyone in D.C. as long as we're here. Those were my only fucking rules, and you went and broke them the first time I turned my back."

"You want to talk about breaking rules?" she retorted. "I seem to remember someone trying to make an escape the other day."

Fuck. Should've known that would come back to bite him in the ass. "Key difference, I didn't leave. As much as I wanted to, as much as I needed to get out, get some air, I stopped myself. As you should've when you picked up that phone to call your office."

"Dammit, I have to work."

Frustration, worry, and anger brewed into an explosive combination in his chest, and he grabbed her by the shoulders, hauling her out of her chair. He couldn't figure out which he wanted to do more: kiss her sassy mouth shut or shake some goddamn sense into her hard head. "You're on vacation!"

With a jerk of her shoulders, she dislodged his hands and dropped back into her seat like she had every intention of returning to the legal brief on screen. "I don't *take* vacations."

Jude yanked the computer's plug out of the wall. "Explains why you're such an uptight hard-ass."

She whirled in the chair to face him again. "I'm the hard-ass? Excuse me, but *I* didn't just toss *your* four-hundred-dollar phone into a pool for breaking the so-called rules."

"Those so-called rules are in place to keep you in one piece."

"For godsakes, I was talking to Noah."

"Who could be your stalker."

"What about K-Bar?"

"I'm not ruling anybody out. Didn't Noah start working for you around the same time you got the first doll?"

Her mouth opened. Closed after a heartbeat without uttering a sound. For a moment, genuine fear shone on her face, and his anger drained away.

"I'm sorry about the phone," he said as gently as he could manage and ran a hand down the silken length of her ponytail. "But I couldn't risk someone—like Noah—tracking you with it."

"No." She squeezed her eyes shut, shook her head. When her lids lifted, she was all fire and outrage again. "You're wrong. Noah's as harmless as a bunny."

Jude snorted in disbelief. "Yeah, sure. I've never met a lawyer who doesn't have teeth."

"That's just it. Noah's a smart kid, but you need more than brains to get anywhere in big city law, and he's not cut out for it. After he finishes school, he's probably going to end up as a small-town lawyer, handling wills and civil cases. He doesn't have the fortitude for criminal trials."

Christ, she had a counter-response for every point he made. He supposed that was a sign she was good at her job, but it also made it frustrating as hell to carry on a conversation with her. "Libs, think about it. Paper dolls? Is that really something a hardcore gangbanger like K-Bar is going to mess around with? No. It's more like something a kid with no backbone would do."

Libby brightened. "Exactly! That's what I've been trying to tell you all along. K-Bar's not involved, and the notes and dolls are just some nutso's ridiculous idea of a joke." She made a move like she was going to stand. "So now that you finally get it, why don't we just end this nightmare of a vacation and go home? We'll never have to see each other again."

He kept her in the chair with a hand on her shoulder. "Yeah, nice try, babe. Even if it's not K-Bar, there's still a very real threat that we need to take seriously."

Her lower lip trembled into something damn close to a pout, though he bet she'd kick him in the balls if he pointed it out. Still, he couldn't resist the urge to drag his thumb over the inviting jut of her lip.

"Someone tried to run you over, remember?"

She turned away, and damn it all to hell, even though it was just one more rejection in a very long line of many, it stung. Way more than it should have.

"I'm still convinced it was you they were aiming for," she said, all prim and haughty like a princess addressing a servant so far beneath her that he barely rated her notice.

All right. If she wouldn't accept tender words or gestures from him, he could go back to being the hard-ass. He crossed his arms over his chest and stared down at her. "We're staying until your father or my brothers give me the all clear to take you back."

With a groan, she banged her forehead on the desk. Once. Twice. Damn woman was going to give herself a concussion.

Jude winced. Squatting beside her, he caught her chin in his hand to stop her from doing it again. "C'mon, it's not that bad. If your father had it his way, we'd be shacked up in some cabin on a dead-end mountain road, trying not to freeze to death. At least here you can enjoy some sun, the pool—"

"And your shining presence?" she said, heavy on the sarcasm.

"I can tell ya my presence is a lot more shiny here than it woulda been in that mountain cabin."

"Small consolation." She sighed and lifted her head. "Do we have any wine? I have a headache."

"You bang your head on a desk and expected *not* to have a—" Jude wisely sealed his lips when her eyes narrowed in warning. He hitched a thumb toward the kitchen. "I stuck a bottle in the fridge to chill for you."

"Look at that." She patted his cheek in the same

indulgent way his mother had when he was five and had drawn himself a report card to go with his brothers' already pinned to the fridge. "You can be tamed after all."

Jude stayed where he was for a moment after she got up and walked toward the kitchen.

Tamed? Him?

Nah, he decided and stood. He hadn't been tame a day in his life and didn't plan to be. Someone out of the five Wilde boys had to live up to the name, after all.

Chapter Thirteen

"Another glass already?"

Libby glared up at him as he walked into the kitchen from the living room, where he'd been watching TV. Then, just to be pissy, she dumped more of the wine into her glass. He held up his hands in surrender. "Just asking."

"It's not like I have any work to do. I'm on *vacation*."

He exhaled. "You're going to be pissed about that for days, aren't you?"

"Hmm." She swirled her wine, pretended to consider it. "Yeah, I think so. And you owe me a new phone."

He waved a dismissive hand and disappeared into the bedroom. Impossible man. Impossible, frustrating man. With a shake of her head, she stuffed the cork back into the neck of the wine bottle and returned to her seat at the kitchen island, where she'd left her book open on the countertop. She started reading, intent on sinking back into the words and forgetting about him for a while, but a thump from the bedroom drew her attention. Another thunk. An exclamation.

What the hell was he doing in there?

She stood and made it halfway to the hall when he reappeared with a box in his hands. He breezed past her and deposited his cargo on the dining table in the open area between the kitchen and living room.

As she moved to his side, she got a good look at the box. "Battleship?"

"My favorite. I knew Seth had some board games stashed away somewhere from when his family used to use this place as a vacation house, but I didn't think I'd find this one. Wanna play?"

"Seriously?"

"We don't have anything else to do," he said with mock gravity. "We're on vacation."

"Yes, ha-ha, throw my words back at me. You're so clever. Let's all laugh." She traced her nail along the edge of the old, beat-up box. "I haven't played this since I was… I don't know. Ten?"

"Really?" Jude seemed genuinely surprised as he opened the box and handed her one of the game boards. "The twins and I play all the time. It's our go-to game when we're bored."

"But…you're adults."

"So?" With that, he pulled out a chair, sat down, and focused on placing his ships. She watched him for a moment, amazed at the pure enjoyment he got out of finding the perfect position for each of his game pieces. He muttered to himself—a mix of "hmm" and "nope" and "ah-ha!" until he was finally satisfied and gazed up. He frowned when he realized she still hadn't opened her board. "You don't want to play?"

Sighing, she gave in. Like he said, it wasn't as if she had anything else to do. She retrieved her wine from the island, then sat down across from him. Opening her board, she took considerably less time placing her ships.

His frown only deepened. "You're supposed to strategize. That's part of the fun."

"I did."

He made a face.

"I did!" she insisted.

"Uh-huh. You're making this too easy."

"I am not!"

"All right, then how about we up the ante?"

"I'm not betting on a children's game."

"No betting. Well, not really." A smile—that damned quicksilver grin she found so appealing—twitched at the corner of his mouth. "More like…strip poker. Or in this case, Battleship."

She stared at him.

"What?" he asked, all blue-eyed innocence. "It'll make things interesting. I get a hit, you take off a piece of clothing."

"And vice versa?" she asked.

He chuckled. "Always the negotiating lawyer, huh?"

"It's not fair if the rules only apply to me."

"All's fair in love and Battleship."

"Uh-huh." She picked up her wineglass and pushed away from the table. "I'm not playing."

"Ah, c'mon, Libs. I was joking. Of course the strip rule applies to me, too. It wouldn't be fun otherwise."

Libby knew she was dancing too close to the fire, but

the wine was a warm, heavy buzz in her head, muffling the little voice inside her mind that always told her the proper way to act, the right thing to say. In fact, it felt good to ignore that annoying voice. And, besides, she never could resist a challenge.

She returned to her seat. "All right. Deal."

Jude grinned and waved a hand in a flourish, indicating she should start. "Ladies first."

"Because you are such a gentleman."

He waggled his brows. "We already established that I'm most definitely not."

At the reminder, a hot flush blazed just under the surface of her skin. The wine, she told herself. The sudden jump in the room's temp was only from the wine. Seeing as she was on her second glass, she should probably slow down.

"Well?" Jude prompted. "Give me your best shot."

She emptied her glass and pushed it away before studying her game board. "B-four."

He groaned. "Aw, man. You got—"

"Hah!"

"A miss," he finished with a laugh. "Gotcha."

She grabbed a white peg. "You suck."

"Only when asked, babe."

Okay, *that* rush of heat had nothing to do with the alcohol in her system. That was 150 percent pure lust. Her imagination went wild with ideas of places she could ask him to—

Game. They were playing a game. Nothing more.

She forced her attention back to the board, but the next three coordinates she tried were misses. Jude got her cruiser on his second try.

"Pay up," he said and held out a hand. She reached down

and pulled off one of her socks, then held it out to show she had indeed taken off an article of clothing.

He scowled and looked under the table. "Damn. I didn't know you were wearing those."

She just smiled sweetly and set the sock aside. "I seem to have the advantage. You're wearing a lot less than I am."

"That's not gonna make any difference."

"Mmm." She eyed him over the edge of her game board. "We'll see."

"Oh, it's on now." He cracked his knuckles and got down to the business of sinking her ships one by one. With each new hit, she lost another article of clothing, but it was sort worth seeing the hitch in his breathing every time she showed a little more skin.

"You sunk my cruiser." She pouted, but secretly her body thrummed as he sat back with one arm slung across the chair next to him and scanned her with heavy-lidded eyes.

"Shorts," he said.

"Cocky," she shot back.

His arm left the back of the chair and dipped beneath the table. "Uh-huh. I am that."

Her own breath caught at the mental image of what he was doing to himself under there, which made him grin and release his hold on himself.

"Shorts," he said again.

Oh, he wanted her shorts? Fine. She stood and gave him her back, hooking her thumbs in the elastic waistband. Slowly, so very slowly, she wiggled out of them, then bent over with her ass in the air to take them off her feet. He groaned. Satisfied with that response, she straightened and faced him in just her tank top, one sock, and her panties.

Eyes smoldering with barely banked lust, he stared like he was trying to photograph her with his mind. She had to battle the ridiculous urge to throw herself at him and ride him until they broke the chair.

Dammit. She was supposed to be teaching him a lesson with this strip tease, not torturing herself.

She dropped into her seat and finished her wine in a gulp, hoping to cool the wildfire he'd ignited in her, then made herself refocus on the game. "A-eight."

Even though she wasn't looking at him, she heard the devastating smile in his voice when he said, "Miss."

By the time she had only her battleship standing, she'd talked herself into another glass of wine and was feeling flushed despite the fact that she was down to her bra and underwear. She still hadn't found even one of Jude's ships.

"You're cheating," she insisted, squinting at him through blurry eyes. "Are you moving them around?"

He held up his hands. "I swear I'm not."

"Uh-huh. Then how come you're still dressed?"

"I'm just that good. A-six."

"Hit. Dammit." She placed the red peg in her battleship, then stared down at herself. Bra or panties? She decided on her bra and reached around to unclasp it, but Jude stopped her.

"Uh-uh," he said, voice thick. "Panties first."

"You can't be serious."

Heat sparked in his gaze. "Absolutely."

"Fine." She stretched out her legs and shimmied out of the panties before balling them up in her hand. She tossed them at him. They bounced off his chest. Laughing, he scooped them up with his finger and waved them like a victory flag. She laughed, too. Couldn't help it. He looked so damn satisfied with himself.

"I should forfeit," she told him.

"You won't."

"You're going to win."

"Yup," he said, completely unapologetic.

And a moment later he did, sinking the battleship and taking her bra as a prize. She hadn't scored even one hit against him. How was that possible? She stood and leaned over the table to peek at his board. All of his ships sat stacked one on top of each other.

"You did cheat, you jerk!"

"No, I took a calculated risk. If you had hit one of my ships, you would have hit them all."

"I demand a rematch!"

He smirked and reached out to trail a finger along the curve of her breast. "You don't have any more clothes."

"I'll play naked."

"Now that's an intriguing offer."

And a stupid one. Why the hell had that popped out of her mouth? It must be a mix of the wine and her competitive nature getting the best of her, and she reeled herself in, sat back down, and crossed her arms over her breasts. "That wasn't a fair game."

"Fair enough."

"Ugh. You're infuriating."

"And you're beautiful."

That stopped her indignation in its tracks, and she realized he was staring at her like he wanted to lick her all over, all but devouring her with his eyes. Heat bloomed under her skin. Her nudity hadn't bothered her before, but she didn't want him to see the flush, didn't want to let him know how much that languorous sweep of his heavy-lidded blue eyes turned her on. She scrambled to find something to cover herself with, ended up grabbing the thin blanket draped over the back of the nearby couch, and clutched it to herself as she stood.

"We had our one night," she reminded him, and his easy smile slipped away.

"I'm not satisfied with that."

"Too bad."

Jude's jaw tightened until a tick started in his cheek. "Are you?"

"That was the deal."

"Forget the damn deal. You know how good we are together, Libby."

They were good together, but only in bed, and that was the problem. If he were any other man, she'd have indulged in a fling without a thought. Then again, if he were any other man, she wouldn't have been interested in a fling to begin with. Jude was it for her. The first time they had made love, he'd ruined her for all other men, and she'd made her peace with the fact that she was going to end up a career-focused spinster.

Now here he was again. Back in her life, offering only part of what she truly wanted, and she couldn't bring herself to take even that. She couldn't put herself through the heartbreak of falling in love with him again, and she was terrified that she wouldn't be able to help herself if she spent more than one night with him.

Shaking her head, she backed away. "I can't. I'm sorry."

Chapter Fourteen

Libby rolled over on the big bed for the fourth time that night and kicked off the sheets. So uncomfortable. And hot, her skin flushed despite the softly blowing air conditioner.

Why couldn't she just sleep already?

Okay, she knew that answer even though she loathed admitting it, even to herself. Every time she closed her eyes, she saw images of Jude in this bed with her, doing things to her that made her insides quake.

It wasn't fair.

Out of all the men on the planet, she had to want the one who was the worst for her mental health. Frustrating, annoying, impossible, selfish Jude Wilde.

But he was right about one thing: they burned up the sheets together and, God, did she need the release of a good orgasm right now. She'd been wound so tight since their fight this afternoon, and then the way he'd stared at her during

Battleship...

No man ever stared at her like that. No man, that is, except for Jude.

"You can't have him," she told the ceiling.

Well, no, that wasn't completely true. She couldn't let herself have the *real* him again—but the fantasy version, the one she kept locked away in her mind and brought out on lonely nights? That version of Jude she'd permit herself. He'd always be there, always be hers, and he was perfect because he never spoke. Never teased. Never infuriated. He was just there to offer pleasure.

She closed her eyes, and as she traced a hand down her body, she pictured him, the Jude she used to know. Younger, his hair shorter in a severe military cut, his body leaner and less muscled. No earring. No tattoos. Same pale blue eyes, quick smile, and talented fingers.

She imagined those fingers now, slick with her desire, parting her folds, finding her clitoris. Her body tightened as pleasure zinged through her, and a low moan escaped her throat. He slid a finger into her, testing her, and she was oh so ready, hanging on by a thread. His thumb tweaked her bundle of nerves, and his lips brushed her neck, traced her jaw.

Come for me, babe. Now. I want you to come for me.

Oh God. Young Jude faded away as the words whispered through her mind and an image of the man sleeping out on the couch took his place.

Come for me.

She was going to, her body trembling on the edge of that abyss. Holy hell, this fantasy was so much more potent. Jude, with his earring and all his tattoos, his wide shoulders and hard body that always crushed her into the mattress with each powerful thrust of his hips. She strained toward climax, begging him to finish it, to take her over into oblivion with his amazing fingers — and still it wasn't enough.

Dammit. Fantasy wasn't enough.

Nearly sobbing in frustration, she lifted her hips to meet her hand and squeezed her eyes shut tighter. She needed to come. She needed…

"Jude." Yes, saying his name helped. He was right there in bed with her, driving her mercilessly toward orgasm, whispering naughty things in her ear. "Jude…" So close, her thighs quivered and her inner muscles clenched around her fingers. But it…wasn't…enough. "Jude!"

At the shout from the bedroom, Jude shot to instant wakefulness and grabbed his firearm from the end table where he'd set it before stretching out for the night.

Something was wrong. Libby wouldn't call out for him. Not unless something bad was happening.

He didn't waste time dressing and ghosted toward the bedroom, pushing open the door as silently as possible. If someone was in there with her, he wanted some element of surprise—

He ground to a halt and stared at the bed, his mouth suddenly dry as he engaged his weapon's safety and placed it on the nearby dresser. Libby lay splayed out on top of the sheets, her nightshirt bunched up around her shoulders, giving him a prime view of her body. Her hand stroked between her legs, her slender fingers sinking in and out of her sex, and she arched with the movement, her eyes screwed shut, her body taut. Struggling for a climax, she needed somebody to give her a little something more, somebody to love her right, to raise her up and over the mental block keeping her from coming.

That someone should be him. Always him. *Only* him.

Fucking hell.

All the blood drained from his head at that possessive thought, making him dizzy as fuck, and his erection jumped from half-mast to ahoy matey so fast he nearly exploded right then and there. He dipped a hand inside his shorts and gripped himself to stop it from happening, squeezed until the line between pleasure and pain blurred, and a groan rumbled from his chest without his consent.

Libby's eyes snapped open. "Oh God! What are you doing in here?"

"You called for me."

"You're crazy. I wouldn't—" She started to sit up and withdraw her hand, but Christ, he couldn't let her. He wanted to watch her pleasure herself more than he'd ever wanted anything in his life.

"Don't." His voice was pure gravel, but he didn't bother clearing his throat. He pumped his hand up and down his shaft in hard strokes. "Let me see you. I need to see you."

Her gaze drifted down his body, her eyes widening at the sight of his straining cock. After a second that seemed to last for years, she slowly settled back against the pillows and let her knees fall open. Her hand returned to her pretty pink sex, and as he watched her dip her fingers inside herself, his whole body started to tremble.

"I did call for you," she admitted and dropped her head

back to stare at him through heavy-lidded eyes. "I was imaging you doing this, your fingers right here where mine are, stroking me."

He couldn't find his voice, couldn't tear his gaze away from the slow slide of her fingers in and out. Unconsciously, he matched his strokes to her rhythm.

"I want you," she gasped, and he saw he wasn't the only one trembling. As her thumb pressed against her clit, her legs shook so hard she vibrated the bed. "I want you, and I know I shouldn't. I can't help myself."

"You want me?" He was panting now, about to go off like a teenager making out in the backseat of his first car. He wanted to be inside her when he did, and it took every ounce of control he could muster not to jump onto that bed and pound into her until they were both screaming. "Say the word, Libs. That's all you gotta do."

She caught his gaze, held it. "Yes."

He dove for the nightstand and yanked open the drawer for the condoms he'd stored there during their first night in Key West. As he ripped one open and covered himself, Libby's velvet laugh was more seductive than a caress. It rippled down his spine and tightened his balls, leaving him breathless and desperate to plunge into her body.

But not yet. Not quite yet.

He grabbed her ankles and pulled her across the bed. Rough. Too rough, and yet he couldn't seem to slow it down, take it easy. He held her open, looped her legs over his shoulders, and bent to taste her. Just a quick taste for now—he already wasn't going to last long and needed inside her.

Libby cried out and bucked against his mouth, her legs going rigid around his shoulders as the orgasm she'd been striving for slammed through her, leaving her gasping, the muscles in her thighs quivering. He gave her clit one last tease with his tongue, then stood and buried himself all the way inside her in one hard plunge. Again. And again. She screamed his name with her next climax, and the sound shattered his control. He leaned over her, planted his hands by her hips for better leverage and pumped hard, driving in as deep as he could get. His release surged out of him with so much power, he half feared his cock had exploded.

Breathing ragged, sweat chilling his overheated skin, he fell forward, catching himself on his forearms and resting his head on her breasts. His feet were still flat on the floor, but with the way his damn legs trembled, he didn't think he'd be able to lift his weight off her for…oh, never. Her heart hammered under his ear, and he smiled sleepily at the sound.

"Can you move?" Libby finally said. "I need water."

Oh shit. She didn't sound content. More like annoyed. Had he done something wrong? He wracked his lust-addled brain for any hint that he'd screwed up. She'd said yes, and he knew she'd come at least twice before he'd lost himself in his own pleasure and quit counting. Maybe she'd been faking…but he didn't think so. Nobody could fake the involuntary muscle spasms that had squeezed his cock so hard that he'd been unable to hold back his own orgasm.

"Yeah. Sorry." He willed his still trembling muscles to work and straightened, realizing too late that he was still inside her. He hissed as their bodies dislodged, and she let out a soft moan.

Son of a bitch, he was already getting hard again. He watched Libby walk toward the master bath until the door closed behind her, then disposed of the condom and sat down on the bed, making himself comfortable with a pillow behind his back. With a mix of wonder and disgust at himself, he stared down his body at his cock, which was definitely up for a round two.

That woman. Christ, he must be a glutton for punishment because he just couldn't get enough.

When the door opened again, she stood silhouetted by the bathroom lights, wrapped up in a short robe that looked silky to the touch. He wanted to take that soft tie off the robe and wind it around her wrists. Or, hell, she could even tie him up with it. Actually, that thought was far too appealing, and he covered himself with his hands to hide his instant reaction.

Unmoving, she stared at him from the doorway for a long time.

Jude winced at the expression on her face. "Are you gonna pull out the 'this was mistake' line and kick me back to the couch?"

She rolled her bottom lip through her teeth, but then shook her head. "No, not this time. We're both adults now. We should be able to carry on a physical affair."

"A physical affair," he echoed. Was she saying...? No way. She couldn't be. He must have misunderstood or something. Then again, there wasn't much in her statement to misunderstand. "Uh, lemme make sure I'm hearing you right. Just for the sake of clarity. You want to keep having sex?"

"We may be here for a while. It's logical, as long as we keep emotions out of it."

Jude blinked. This was too good to be true. "No emotions?"

"None," she agreed and moved to sit on the end of

the bed. "Just sex. There's no denying the chemistry we have in bed, so why not exploit it? At very least, it's a nice distraction."

Nice distraction. Those oh-so-logical words tweaked something a little too close to his heart for comfort, so he did what he always did when something hurt: he grinned. "Well, hell. What kind of a man would I be if I said no to that deal?"

Chapter Fifteen

No news. Save for the incessant calls from the damn lawyer for updates to give Pruitt, nothing much was happening.

Jude sighed, pocketed his phone, and continued pacing the house. Part of him—Libby would say the insane part of him—almost wished something would happen with K-Bar already. Even with their mutually satisfying nights together, the days were beginning to seem endless, and sitting around the house waiting for an anvil to drop on their heads was starting to grate on his nerves. Libby's, too, if he had to guess by the way she'd gone all neat-freak on him. The woman had spent almost every waking moment scrubbing, mopping, and dusting, and last night he'd noticed the effects of all that hard work in her chapped hands and ragged fingernails. He kept expecting her to run out of things to clean, but she always managed to find something else, so this morning, he'd suggested she relax and read another book. That had not gone over well. She'd thrown it in his face that she wouldn't have to clean every day if he didn't make such a mess all of the time.

"What mess?" he'd demanded incredulously, pulled off the basketball shorts he liked to sleep in, and tossed them aside while he rooted around in his drawer for a pair of board shorts for his morning swim. "The place is cleaner now than when we arrived."

"*Your* mess!" She scooped up his shorts and stuffed them in the hamper along with her nightshirt. She looked gorgeous standing there in her bra and panties and nothing else, but he was too annoyed to act on his cock's interest.

"I don't make a mess."

"Uh, yes, you do. You take off your clothes and leave them where they land."

Okay, she got him there. "I pick them up eventually."

"Eventually's not soon enough!" She snatched a sock from the floor by the end of the bed and thrust it at him. "I purposely left this laying on the floor, waiting to see if you'd pick it up."

Outrage burned through him as he slammed the dresser drawer shut and spun to face her. "You *tested* me?"

"Uh-huh. And you failed miserably."

"No shit. I didn't see it there."

"That's the problem. You never see any of it. Know how long this sock has been there? Hm? Three days, Jude. Three. Days." She threw the sock into the hamper with everything else. "And that's not even the half of it. You have no clue how to run the dishwasher. You leave toothpaste in the sink. You—"

"All right, since you're Ms. Spic-and-Span herself." He

motioned toward the en suite. "You wanna tell me why you have every hair product known to mankind scattered on the bathroom counter?"

"Because that's where they belong!"

"But my shave kit belongs under the sink?"

"Yes!"

That had sparked another round of bickering, which ended with her shoving him out of the bedroom and shutting herself in to organize their socks by type and color or some shit. Jude left her alone to go for his morning swim, but two hours later, he was all but climbing the walls. When he realized he'd just completed his fifth lap around the living room furniture, he stopped and shook his head.

Something had to change. Like, right now. They needed a break, some kind of release valve, or they were going to end up driving each other into straitjackets.

Drive.

Now there was an idea. Technically, they should stay in the house, but fuck it. This wasn't witness protection. Since he'd heard nothing from nobody about anything for three long days, a drive wouldn't hurt. And…maybe a picnic somewhere remote and quiet, away from the constant crowd of tourists on Key West. Someplace where the only possible threat to Libby would be a sunburn.

Yeah, he liked this idea. He took a moment to let a plan solidify in his mind, then pulled out his phone again. He knew just the place.

L ibby had to admit it felt incredible to be out of that house and among the bustle of civilization again. As Jude navigated the rented convertible through traffic, the hotels alongside the road gave way to condos and then to nontouristy commercial and residential properties. Finally, civilization surrendered to marshlands, and she started to fidget as paranoia gnawed at the back of her brain.

"Where are we going?" He'd said they were only going for a drive around the island, but the car seemed to be pointed away from Key West.

Jude glanced over the tops of his sunglasses with that panty-melting smile of his, but gave no other answer. He just stepped on the gas and turned up the radio as Bob Marley told them not to worry about a thing. The convertible cleared the edge of the island, and nothing but water and sky and miles of highway stretched before them. Wind whipped her hair into a frizzy mess, but suddenly she didn't care.

Beautiful.

No, wait. With the sun dancing over the calm, crystalline ocean's surface, "beautiful" didn't even come close to describing it. Stunning was a better word. Gorgeous. Breathtaking.

Libby lifted her face to the sky, the sun warm on her cheeks, and inhaled the salt-rich air. Her lungs expanded for what felt like the first time in her life. It was like flying, and she had the strangest urge to unbuckle, stand up, and embrace the heady sensation of freedom with her entire being.

"Do it."

She whipped around in her seat to stare at Jude. "What?"

"You want to stand up, do it."

"No! Are you crazy?"

"Depends on your definition." He grinned again. "And I know you have a wild and crazy woman buried in there somewhere. I get a peek at her every night, remember?"

The back of her neck burned at the reminder. "That's different."

"How? C'mon, unleash her again for me," he cajoled in a soft, seductive voice she almost couldn't hear over the wind. "You don't have to wait until sex to let it all go."

Oh, was she ever temped, except… She hadn't done anything wild or reckless since he left and wasn't about to start now just because he was back in her life for a short time. "It's dangerous."

"Life's no fun without a little danger. C'mon, Libs. Double dog dare you."

"You didn't just say that."

"Triple," he challenged.

She stared at him in utter disbelief. "Are you five?"

"Is that a no? Okay, then I will." He lifted his hands off the steering wheel, gripped the windshield, and hoisted himself up. Libby's heart lurched, and she squeezed her eyes shut, bracing for impact. Horns blared from passing cars, but the convertible didn't smack into anything or drift into oncoming traffic or jump over the concrete side of the bridge and land in the ocean. After a moment, she peeled one eye open. Then the other.

Holy shit. Jude was holding the wheel steady with his legs.

She released a pent-up breath. "You've done this before."

"A few times." He held out a hand. "C'mon. Just for a second. Let yourself enjoy the moment, Libs."

Enjoy the moment. When was the last time she'd let

herself enjoy anything? Aside from sex with him, she honestly couldn't remember. Her life in D.C. revolved around work and more work. Deep down, she knew the stress of it all, the burden she carried to right wrongs day in and day out, was crushing her.

Oh God. Was insanity contagious? Had to be because she was actually going to do this ridiculous stunt.

"Okay." She gulped down her fear, unbuckled her seat belt before she could think better of it, and set her hand in Jude's. He hauled her up and guided her hands to hang on to the windshield, then dropped back into the driver's seat. With a twist of the radio's knob, he sent Bob Marley's words of wisdom soaring.

"Wait, wait, wait. What are you doing?"

"Driving." He stopped her with a hand on her arm as she tried to sit down. "Let it go!"

Wind tore the breath from her lungs and ripped tears from her eyes. She stared in wonder at the Overseas Highway stretching before them, at the ocean, lit with sparks of sunlight, expanding forever on each side of the bridge. On the horizon to the east, she spotted a sailboat cruising toward Key West. To the west, a school of fish jumped into the air, their scales flashing silver before they disappeared under the surface again. It was…wonderful.

Laughter bubbled up from somewhere deep inside of her, and she lifted her arms, let her head fall back, and sang out Bob Marley's lyrics to the sky.

And for the moment, she believed them. Everything was going to be all right.

Chapter Sixteen

Jude jumped aboard the small fishing boat called the *Gladys Marie* and smiled up at Libby, who stood on the dock with an expression of doubt on her face.

"That thing can't possibly be safe."

"Sure it is." He thumped a hand on the boat's railing. "Old Gladys is as sturdy as…uh…" He couldn't think of anything reassuring to compare it to and said, "Well, she's sturdy."

"Maybe so." Libby eyed the platinum-blond kid with the nose ring that was to be their captain. "But I'm more worried about him. Is he even old enough to drive this thing?"

"I'm twenty-one," the kid protested.

Jude shrugged. "See, he's a responsible adult."

Libby snorted but finally relented and grasped his hand. He helped her aboard.

"Where are we going?" she asked for the hundredth time as she sat next to him in the bow.

"On an adventure."

She rolled her lower lip through her teeth. "So I should be worried."

"You'll like it. Promise."

She made a noncommittal sound, dragged her bag onto her lap, and hunted around inside for a moment. She brought out a bottle of SPF 50 sunscreen.

Go figure.

Jude laughed and watched her slather it on, part of him wishing he were the coconut-scented goo she spread so liberally all over her body. She sent him a sidelong glance. "Don't look."

He grinned. "Make me."

"God, you're such a child." With an exasperated exhale, she lifted the edges of her swimsuit top and rubbed the stuff on her breasts.

Oh hell. It took everything he had in him not to groan, and he couldn't help but wonder if the sunscreen tasted as good as it smelled. Was she *trying* to torture him? Knowing her, probably.

"You need to put some on, too," she said in a won't-take-no-for-an-answer tone and held the tube out to him. So, naturally, he had to brush it aside. At this point, poking at her had gone beyond an amusing pastime and into compulsion territory, but he got the feeling she enjoyed their bickering as much as he did.

"I'll be fine."

She sniffed, snapped the tube shut, and dropped it into her bag. "Don't you come whining to me when you're burned to a crisp, buddy. I'll just laugh and do my I-told-you-so dance."

"Now that's something I'd pay to see. Does it involve a

pole?"

She punched him in the shoulder. Hard. "You're an ass."

Satisfied with the outcome of the conversation, he lifted his face to the sun and inhaled the salty air. The ocean was as flat as a sheet of blue glass today, the only waves the ones coming off the boat as she skimmed across the water toward their destination. He stole a glance at Libby. She sat beside him with her eyes closed, her face also raised to the sun and wind. When she smiled, he did, too. She loved this. Sure, she'd cut off her own tongue with nail clippers before she admitted to it, but she was just as taken with the colors and sounds and flavors of the Keys as he was.

He couldn't wait to see what her reaction would be to the afternoon he had planned and all but bounced in his seat with impatience. No doubt she was going to bitch and moan—and he couldn't wait for the argumental gymnastics to follow—but he was also sure she was going to relish every second of it. At least he hoped so. He wanted to see her relax, wanted her to forget for a little while why they were in this tropical paradise. An escape for them both.

Fuck, his nerves were jangling around under his skin like obnoxious church bells.

Unable to stay seated any longer, he got up and paced the length of the boat, rubbing the ring in his shorts pocket like some kind of fucking magic lamp. He stopped and forced himself to remove his hand from the pocket and zip it up so he wouldn't be tempted again. Libby gave him a quizzical look at the sound of the zipper, but went back to enjoying the ride without a word of question.

Hah. The lawyer was speechless. Had to be a first.

Temptation to provoke her again niggled at him, just so

he could watch the flush of debate fill her cheeks. She was beautiful when she went into full lawyer-mode. *Then again,* he thought as she leaned over the railing, her hair loose and dancing around her face like rays of sunlight, *she was always beautiful.*

Nerves again. He rubbed his hands together, told himself to chill the fuck out. It wasn't like he was proposing a second time. She'd probably laugh and kick him in the balls if he tried something that asinine. Still…he wanted everything perfect. Worry-free. And, yeah, maybe a little romantic.

Maybe he'd just check in with the captain one last time to make sure everything was all set.

When the boat slowed and coasted toward one of the little islands they had been circling for the last half hour, Libby sent a questioning glance Jude's way. He merely grinned back.

She rolled her eyes. That man. His grin really shouldn't set off rabbles of butterflies in her stomach.

The boat coasted toward a dock that looked half as sturdy as they one they'd left an hour ago. Jude stood at the bow and leaned out, grabbing ahold of a rope to help guide them in. After tying them with a skillful knot, he turned and reached down a hand to help her up and out.

"Ladies first."

How gentlemanly. Funny thing—he was a gentleman. Two weeks ago, she never would have thought so. But he'd given her a flower every day. He'd found a new copy of her ruined book. He had run out into public half-naked just to keep an overgrown lizard from giving her nightmares. What was all of that if not gentlemanly?

Libby waited on the dock for him to grab his pack and disembark. The captain unloaded a huge surfboard and one long paddle from the back of the boat, then jumped in behind the wheel again and gave a wave. Jude untied the boat, pushed it away from the dock, and waved back.

"Whoa, wait," Libby said, panic rising. "Where is he going?"

"Home." He took her hand and led her toward the beach.

"He's leaving us out here?"

"We have another ride."

"What other ride? No, never mind. I don't want to know the answer just yet. I have a feeling I'm not going to like it. I—oh." She stopped short and stared at the beach, as white as freshly fallen snow. Someone had laid out a green blanket underneath an umbrella the same shade of tropical blue as the sky. On the blanket sat a picnic basket and a metal ice bucket sweating in the heat.

Jude's smile was 100 percent smug male. "Hungry?"

"You set this all up for me?"

"Who else?"

She should smack him for that, should feel outraged that he'd staged this whole cheesy seduction when he knew good and well all he had to do was ask and she'd go to bed with him. But she couldn't find the outrage. She dug deep within herself, and all she came up with was humbled wonder, especially when his smile started to slip and worry furrowed his brow.

"You don't like it."

"No. I mean, yes. Of course I do. It's…it's lovely. And… sweet. So very sweet."

His smile returned, all dazzle and boyish excitement. He entwined his fingers through hers and pulled her toward the picnic. He sat her down on the blanket, dropped his pack on a jutting rock a few feet away, and joined her under the umbrella.

"What would you like?" he asked as he opened the cooler. "I know you hate tomatoes, so I avoided ordering anything with them, but other than that, I was guessing. We have some melon pieces, trail mix, a couple different kinds of sandwiches, some pasta salad—oh, that looks good." He picked up the plastic container and shook it. "I'll have some of this. We also have wine. White. Sorry, not your favorite but it's easier to keep wine chilled out here than at room temperature so I—"

Libby reached across all of the containers and plastic-wrapped packages of food, placed her hand over his, and gave his fingers a light squeeze. "Thank you."

Such insufficient words for the overwhelming affection she suddenly felt toward him, but they would have to do because she couldn't think of any others. Or at least none that wouldn't ruin the moment.

She had to be careful. Affection was a slippery slope. One wrong step and she'd fall headlong into love with this man again, and she refused to take that risk a second time. Even though, in moments like this, it seemed like a perfect idea, a real-life happily ever after…

She twisted her cover identity's simple wedding band around on her finger. It wasn't real. None of this was. She just had to keep reminding herself—

"Fuck!"

Libby jumped and stared in wide-eyed shock as Jude scrambled backward, his hand flailing around behind him for something to grab. Fearing the worst, she searched for the cause of his outburst and found it in the form of a little long-legged spider crawling across the blanket. She looked at him. Then at the spider. Then at him again. And she burst out laughing.

"Seriously?" She cupped her hands around the little thing before he could crush it like he so obviously wanted to. "You'll pick up a giant lizard without a second's thought, but you're afraid of the itsy bitsy spider?"

"You're afraid of a gentle lizard," he shot back, "but you'll pick up a killer spider?"

"Oh, don't be ridiculous. Killer spider," she scoffed. "It's harmless!"

"Yeah, right. Tell that to me when it bites you, and I have to swim your dying ass to the nearest hospital."

Shaking her head, she stood with the spider still clasped in her palms. "I'll let it go."

"Way down the beach." He pointed. "I mean waaaay down."

"Wuss."

"Hey, did I cast stones when I had to save you from the iguana?"

"No, but that doesn't make you any less of a wuss." She left him and let the spider go on a tree branch fifty yards away. When she got back, Jude handed her a glass of wine and wouldn't meet her eyes.

"All right, Mr. Nature Lover," she said after a moment of awkward silence. "Want to tell me what that was about?"

He took great care in pouring his own glass, but still wouldn't meet her gaze.

"Well?" she prompted.

"I feel ridiculous."

"You should." And she probably shouldn't take so much delight in the fact that his ears had turned bright red, but… honestly, it was adorable. She would have dialed down her teasing if he wasn't laughing at himself right along with her. "You screamed like a little girl."

"Bullshit." He finally looked up with an expression of mock horror. "It was a manly scream."

"Very manly," she said and patted his hand.

"All right, you got me. I have a small phobia when it comes to spiders." He removed her hand from his and pointed to an oblong scar on the back of his right hand between his thumb and forefinger. Indented like a shallow crater and puckered around the edges, she remembered she used to rub her thumb over that scar whenever they held hands.

She narrowed her eyes at him. "You told me one of your brothers bit you during a fight."

"It was a better story than getting bit by a spider when I was eight and having a bad reaction," he admitted. "I ended up in the hospital for a week with the skin on my hand split open to the bone."

She winced at that gruesome mental image. For an eight-year-old, it must have been terrifying. "What kind of spider does that much damage?"

"The doctors thought it was a brown recluse, but we never found the spider to know for sure. Ever since…" He shuddered. "No thanks. I'll take my chances with iguanas over spiders any day."

"Fair enough," she said with a smile and sipped her wine. "I'll be your spider slayer if you keep all reptiles far away from me."

He reached over their picnic to shake her hand. "Deal. Now dig in. I have more planned for today."

"I can't wait." She'd meant it as a sarcastic remark, but it hadn't come out sounding like one, and it was the truth—she *was* intrigued to see what he had up his sleeve next.

She watched him dig into the pasta salad with relish and decided on some of the melon slices to go with her own sandwich. As she ate, she mused over how little she actually knew about the man seated across from her attacking his lunch with all the grace of a ravenous animal. She'd dated him for a whole year, and she'd never known about his spider phobia. Made her wonder what else she didn't know about him.

He finished eating before she was even halfway through her sandwich and lounged back on one elbow, his wineglass still in hand. He released a contented sigh and stared out over the ocean. "I could sit here all day."

She followed his gaze over the glittering stretch of paradise laid out before them like a feast for their eyes alone. "It's so quiet here. Peaceful."

"Mmm."

"I can almost pretend I really am on vacation instead of hiding out from some crazy stalker."

"No." He held up a finger. "We're not discussing that. We *are* on vacation today."

"Thank you."

"Why are you thanking me? This is all purely for selfish reasons. I was going stir-crazy and needed out of that house."

"I think we both needed this. I mean, we fought over a sock like an old married couple." As soon as the words left her mouth, she wished she could recall them, but Jude seemed not to notice how awkward those words were. Or maybe he just chose to ignore it.

Ignoring it worked for her. She gulped the rest of her wine. Yes, ignoring worked just fine for her.

In a surge, Jude sat up and started packing his garbage into the picnic basket.

"Where are you going?" she asked when he stood and grabbed his pack.

"The dock."

"What about all this?" She waved a hand at the remnants of their picnic.

"The charter company will clean it all up. It's what they do." He held out a hand and wiggled his fingers. "So how about it? Ready for our next adventure?"

"Probably not." She popped one more slice of melon in her mouth before accepting his hand. "But someone has to keep you out of trouble."

And there it was, that quick, rabble-inducing grin again. "Aw, babe," he said and pulled her to her feet. "Impossible task. Trouble and me, we go way back."

Chapter Seventeen

"You want me to balance on *that*?" Standing on the dock in her swimsuit with her arms crossed over her chest, Libby stared at the rented paddleboard like it was a cousin of her dreaded iguana. "Um, no. I don't think so. Have you met me? I trip over my own feet on a daily basis."

Jude laughed. She was adorable when she stared at him like he was insane. "It'll be fun."

"Says the man who thinks near death experiences are fun."

"C'mon, have I steered you wrong yet?"

She opened her mouth. Closed it after a second without uttering a sound. "No. And I wish I could say otherwise, dammit." She eyed the board again. "Is it safe?"

"You stood up in a moving car on the highway," he reminded her. "You got this."

When she didn't move, he jumped into the water and pulled himself up onto the board, which was much longer and wider than a surfboard and easier to balance on. He held out a hand. "Trust me."

"Never."

Ouch. But, yeah, nothing less than he deserved. "You can sit in front and relax. I'll do the paddling."

She glanced around the deserted beach. "Do I have any other choice?"

"Well, you could sit here by yourself for four hours until I reach the rental place and have them send a boat back."

"Like I said, do I have a choice?" She set her hand in his and stepped off the dock with all the grace of a dropped rock. The board flipped, and she landed in the water with a shriek. Jude laughed so hard he sucked in a lungful of water when he went under and came up coughing.

"Not funny." She splashed him. "You said it was safe."

"It is, but you can't jump on the board like you're pole vaulting." He swam over to her and tugged the rope attached to his ankle, dragging the board close. "Climb on."

"How?"

"Like you would pull yourself out of a swimming pool. Use your legs. I'll keep it steady. Once you get up there, lay flat on your stomach." He bit the inside of his cheek as he watched her struggle. He should probably swim around and give her a helping boost, but...nah. He kind of liked the view from this angle. Her swimsuit top slipped low as she struggled to pull herself up with her arms, giving him a tantalizing peek-a-boo glimpse of her nipple. He wondered how she'd react if he leaned across the board, shoved aside the triangle of black fabric, and sucked that rosy bud into his mouth. She'd probably slap him, but damn, would it be worth it. He'd just about convinced himself to do it when she finally managed to get up on her belly.

She looked good lying there like that, her bare back and legs glistening in the sun as she tried to catch her breath.

"Wow," she breathed and finally lifted her head. "I'm out of shape."

Not from where he stood. You ask him, those two dimples in her back at the base of her spine all but begged for exploration by his lips and tongue.

"Uh...Jude?"

"Yeah." He cleared his throat and willed his half-mast erection to play nice. "Yeah, sorry. Hold on to the board. It's going to shake a little." With a lot less struggle, he climbed on and positioned himself on his knees, one of each side of her waist.

"You made that look too easy," she accused.

Easy. Right. Except he underestimated how difficult sitting in this position was going to be. If he leaned back, even a little, his balls brushed the sweet curve of her ass and every muscle in his body clenched in anticipation.

Okay. They had to get to prime water before he exploded. He maneuvered over to the dock, grabbed his pack and the paddle. He looped the pack across his back, then started paddling in a steady rhythm, moving them away from the choppy water by the dock. Once they were far enough into the calm of the bay, he slowed to a stop and used his weight to steady the board.

"Go ahead and sit up now. Slowly."

She sat up, cross-legged, and he climbed to his feet behind her.

She glanced back. "Am I supposed to stand?"

"Only if you want to."

She bit her lower lip, and he thought she might take the risk. But then, in typical Libby fashion, she shook her head. "I don't think so."

"Your loss." He dug the paddle into the water, propelling them toward the nearby mangrove tunnels. He had to duck under the first low-hanging branch, but then the branches stretched into a green canopy overhead. Gnarled mangrove roots framed the narrow channel, and the only noise came from the slosh of his paddle and the distant call of a bird.

"Are there crocodiles in here?" Libby whispered.

"Doesn't matter."

"It's a valid question. I can't see through the water anymore. Don't they hide in places like this?"

Jude stopped paddling and released a frustrated breath. "I already told you crocs aren't usually found this far south. Besides, you're missing the whole point of this."

Tilting her head back, she stared up at him with real confusion. "What point? Are you *trying* to get us eaten?"

"Libs." He knelt down and balanced the paddle across his knees. She let out a little gasp and gripped the sides of the board as it swayed with his movement.

"I want to go back."

"In a minute." He rubbed her shoulders, felt the hard knots of tension bunched there, and worked them out with his thumbs. "Relax. Look around. What do you see?"

"What do I see? Those creepy, twisted trees you see in swamps and horror movies. Dark water, and who knows what's swimming under us right now. I see a swarm of mosquitoes buzzing away up ahead. We're probably both going to get eaten alive, if not by the crocodiles hiding under those trees, then by the damn bugs. And I bet there are spiders here. That little one was one thing, but if we run into anything bigger, you're on your own, pal."

His Libby, always a pessimist. He leaned in close, putting his lips next to her ear. "You know what I see? I see life. Beautiful, mysterious, and sometimes frightening life. There are so many ugly places and people in this world, I've learned you have to grab hold of the places like this, the moments like this, and cherish them."

Chapter Eighteen

Libby turned her head and found his lips less than an inch from hers. Stunned, she studied his face. His eyes were so serious and a little sad, and she wondered why she'd never noticed that sorrow in him before. Maybe he was just that good at hiding under a gloss of devil-may-care attitude. Or maybe she'd never really looked. Probably more like it. At one time, the wildness in him had thrilled her, and she hadn't wanted him to be anything but the irreverent bad boy that her father disapproved of.

"My God," she whispered. "Who are you?"

Confusion carved grooves in his forehead. "I'm…me."

"No, you're not. Not the Jude I knew. That Jude wouldn't care about…" She waved a hand at the scenery, at a loss for words. "Well, any of this. What happened to you to make you change so much?"

"Oh." His shoulders slumped, but then he met her gaze straight on, and she saw a flicker of something there. Hope?

Fear? Maybe an anxious combination of both. "I'm the same guy I've always been, Libby."

"Then I barely knew you. That whole year, you might as well have been a stranger to me." The realization lodged a hard lump in her throat. "It never would have worked between us."

"Probably not," he agreed.

"Did you know that when you proposed to me?"

"I knew you only saw part of me, the part I projected, but I was okay with that. I'm used to being that man and could have kept on being him for you. I've been playing the part most of my life anyway."

"But…" She couldn't wrap her mind around any of this. "Why?"

He shrugged. "Because that's what was expected of me from my brothers, my classmates, my teachers, my superior officers… Jude, the wild child. The perpetual fuck up."

"And you never wanted to prove them wrong?"

"I tried for a while, but in school, if I made good grades, the teachers accused me of cheating. Whenever I tried to help my brothers around home, I always managed to screw shit up. In the Marines, my superiors—your father—labeled me as a problem from day one in OCS and never gave me a shot to prove otherwise. So I stopped trying and let everybody see what they wanted to see."

"Including me."

"Yes. Including you."

She turned away. Stared at the mangroves and their tumble of roots disappearing into the water, almost like they were tiptoeing through the marshlands. She supposed, if she really looked, if she blocked out her fear of the potential threats hiding here, it was kind of beautiful in the same way that Jude was beautiful. Wild, complicated, dangerous — and yet somehow alluring.

She burned to ask him why he'd ended their relationship in the way he had. If he'd wanted out, why hadn't he just walked away? Why had he felt the need to crush her heart into dust first? And so publicly, in front of all of her friends.

Now in this secluded tunnel, miles away from her real life, would be the time to ask if there ever was one, but she couldn't bring herself to form the words. They lodged in her throat. Honestly, she wasn't sure she could bear to hear the answer. "Can we get out of here, please?"

"Yeah. Sure." The board wobbled underneath her as he gained his feet with a fluid grace she envied. The paddle made a soft sound as it dipped into the water and pushed them forward. She watched the mangroves pass overhead in silence, jumping at every little splash against the mangled roots, terrified of a wayward crocodile making them into lunch despite his reassurances.

Jude didn't seem worried. In fact, he was so calm and more relaxed than she had ever seen him. Peaceful. He paddled at an even, steady rhythm, slower than she would have liked, and took in their surroundings with a smile quirking his lips. She found herself watching him more than the scenery.

Eight years ago, she had convinced herself she loved him. If she was honest, under all of the hurt, part of her still felt that way. Except what did she really know about him? He'd all but admitted that the man she knew and once loved was a fantasy version of himself, so who was the real Jude? This one, so serene and carefree, who enjoyed the outdoors? The player who cheated on her with a well-endowed brunette two days after he proposed? Or the man who had asked her to marry him over a romantic dinner with so much emotion that it still choked her up to think about that night?

The quirk of Jude's lips spread into a dazzling smile. He glanced down, caught her gaze with his sparkling baby blues, and motioned up ahead with his chin. "Look."

Still half-afraid of seeing a croc, she slowly turned to face the front of the board, and a gasp escaped her. Up ahead, the mangrove tunnel opened up into an expanse of blue-green ocean. Sunlight shimmered across the top of the calm water, and she shielded her eyes against the brightness.

Now this… This was beautiful. A tropical paradise.

Jude picked up the pace, propelling them away from the shore and the creepy mangroves, out into open water. She was torn between watching the muscles in his arms and chest bunch and flex with each pull of the paddle and the colorful coral reef racing by under the board.

Eventually, they came to a gliding halt. This far out, the white sand beach around the island looked like a rim of salt around a margarita glass, but the water was still fairly shallow and so clear she saw every fish that swam by below them. Jude sat down and laid the paddle alongside his leg, then unzipped the pack that she'd forgotten he still wore. He pulled out two bottles of water, handed her one, and then twisted off the cap of his own. As carefully as she could, she spun around so that she was facing him and watched him drink down the water in three long pulls. Sweat slicked his hair away from his face and made his skin shine in the sunlight.

"This better?" he asked when he finished and reached over his shoulder to return the empty bottle to the bag.

"It's lovely." She finished her own water and handed him the bottle. "It's like nobody's ever been here before."

"And no creepy mangroves." He shifted until he straddled the board, dipping his legs in the water up to just past his knees. Libby bet that felt wonderful and mimicked him, submerging her legs and kicking gently, propelling the board in small circles.

Jude chuckled, took hold of her under her knees, and dragged her toward him. His hands slipped upward, and little thrills zinged from the heat of his palms on her thighs to the tips of her breasts.

"Wanna try something?"

She eyed him, wary of the mischievous sparkle lighting his eyes. "Like what?"

"How good is your balance?"

"Really, you haven't figured that out by now? Not good."

"That's okay. I have enough for the both of us." He pulled her up so that she was straddling him instead of the board, and he nuzzled her cleavage, tugging down the front of her top with his teeth.

"Oh! Oh," she gasped as his lips closed over a taut nipple. "We shouldn't be doing this." And yet she couldn't bear to push him away.

His laughter brushed over her nipple and rumbled through her entire body. "Why not?"

"Because someone—" His thumb slipped under the edge of her swimsuit bottoms and found her clitoris. Pleasure warmed her limbs to pliant rubber. She tightened her legs around him to keep from falling off the board and bit her lip against the need to cry out. "Oh God. Someone could see us."

"So we'll show them how it's done."

"Jude!"

"Libby," he said in the same exasperated tone. "You've stood up in a moving car, gone paddle boarding through the mangroves. You're a regular wild woman. What's another risk? And a little one at that? There's nobody around for miles." His fingers joined his thumb, teasing her entrance but denying her full penetration until her hips bucked, insisting on more.

Male satisfaction tinged his smile. "What do you want?"

"More. Oh God, I want more. What do you do to me?"

"Make you come." His voice was little more than a growl, and he delved his fingers deep into her sex. "Over and over again, I'll make you come."

Her entire being shuddered at his words and the intrusion of his fingers, but it wasn't enough. She needed his body inside hers as she spasmed around him in climax. She reached between them and found his shaft hard, hot, and so ready for her. Wrapping her fingers around him, she squeezed and gave his length a slow, languorous stroke that left him groaning, his free hand clenching in her hair.

"Christ, Libby. Yeah, just like that. Don't stop. Please don't stop." He guided her mouth to his for a branding kiss, and she felt powerful in the most deliciously feminine way, capable of making a strong man like him beg.

"Come here," he whispered against her mouth, and his hands delved under her rear, lifting her up. Balancing her weight with one arm, he shoved down the front of his board shorts, freeing himself. Moisture beaded on the tip of his penis as he took himself in hand. "Reach around into my pack, front left pocket."

She blinked and ripped her gaze away from his hand sliding up and down, up and down. "What?"

"Condoms," he said between his teeth. "We need one."

Wow, he'd thought of everything. She leaned into him and reached over his shoulder, fumbling around to find the right pocket. And maybe she had a little fun teasing him, letting her sex rub against the broad head of his straining erection. The rumble that came from his throat was the most gratifying sound she'd ever heard.

There were at least ten foil packets in the zippered pocket, and she had to laugh. That was her Jude. The eternal optimist.

She handed him one and watched between their bodies as he rolled it on. He held it in place with one hand and guided her hips down with the other.

"Ride me."

Yes. God, yes. In that second, she wanted nothing else.

She dug her nails into his hard shoulders for balance and lowered herself onto him, welcomed him inside her body, rocking until he was as deep as he could go. Then she stilled, enjoying the pulsing, impatient length of him stretching her to the delicious edge between pain and pleasure.

"Babe," he groaned, "you gotta move."

Sweat beaded on his upper lip, the cords in his neck strained at the effort of holding still, and his erection bucked in demand inside her—but she had him trapped, and they both knew it. He had to balance the board so this was 100 percent her show, and call her evil, but she wanted to torture him a bit first.

"I don't *gotta* do anything for you." She wound her fingers in his hair and tugged his lips toward hers, grinding against him in slow circles, letting the sparks of pleasure tingling along her nerve endings guide her movements.

He growled and reached for her waist, but the board started to list to one side. With a curse against her lips, he dropped his hands and readjusted his balance, then scowled at her. "You're enjoying this."

"Yes," she said. "Yes, I am." She lifted her hips until nothing but his tip penetrated her, then sank back onto him with deliberate, agonizing slowness and watched his eyes glaze over with pleasure. "And so are you."

He made a sound close to a whimper as she lifted herself off him again. "You're killing me."

"Then you'll die a happy man."

This time, his laughter came out somewhere between a gasp and a grumble. "You make me so fucking crazy, you know that?"

"Ditto."

She rode him until the tips of her fingers numbed and their breaths mingled in heavy pants. His mouth found her breast again, and the tug of his teeth on her nipple surged all the way to her womb. That was it, all she needed, and her climax shuddered through her in wild bursts of color and sensation that left her in a state of dizzy bliss.

When she opened her eyes again, she realized Jude had taken control, somehow holding the board steady as he grasped her hips and pumped in short, hard strokes. She watched the erotic slide of his body disappearing into hers, saw his sexy stomach muscles convulse just before his head dropped back and he groaned in climax.

Beautiful. Wild, complicated, and dangerous. So very dangerous but now, with her second orgasm building to a shattering peak, she didn't care.

As the electric tingles subsided, she collapsed against him in a clumsy, gasping heap that made the board rock.

"Careful." Jude lifted her and pulled off the condom, sliding it into the package it came in, then dropping it into an empty pocket in his pack for later disposal. He tucked himself back into his shorts before adjusting her bikini bottom, covering her again. She couldn't decide if he was a jerk for worrying about her modesty *now* or if the action was incredibly sweet. Either way, her heart gave a giddy *ba-bump* in response.

With the sigh of well-sated man, Jude settled back on the board, using his pack for a pillow. He pulled her on top of him and draped one arm over his eyes. They lay together like that for a long time, soaking in the warm sun, listening to the soft lap of the water against their board and the guttural *gaw gaw gaw* of birds calling out, almost as if scolding them for their promiscuity. Libby smiled at the thought and lifted her head. They were closer to shore now, had drifted away from the beach and back toward the mangroves, and she could see a handful of black, brown, and yellow birds flitting through the branches. The sun sat lower in the sky, casting deep shadows around the mangrove roots, and worry started to edge out her good mood. She bit her lip. Part of her—the lazy, sun-warmed, sex-sedated part—didn't want today to end, but the rest of her definitely didn't want to be anywhere near those trees after dark.

"We should get back before the sun sets."

Jude gave no reply. She looked down at him.

Sleeping.

Typical man, she thought with amusement. Give 'em an

orgasm and it's lights out. She took a moment to watch the steady rise and fall of his chest, to admire the way the bright red-gold evening sunlight made the ink in his tattoos pop to brilliant life.

Maybe she could get a tattoo. She'd always secretly wanted one and what better time and place to get one than here in this paradise, when her real life felt so far away as to be nonexistent.

But, no, that was ridiculous. Foolish, even. Jude's insanity must be contagious.

She poked him in the ribs and smiled when he grumbled.

"Jude, we need to get moving. I don't want to be out here after dark."

Cracking open one eyelid, he glanced around. "Aw, fuck. You're right." He stretched, yawned. "Hot, mind-blowing sex makes me sleepy."

Libby ignored the flush warming her neck and cheeks. "Will they send someone looking for us if we don't get back to the rental place soon?"

"Probably. But how about we meet them halfway?" After another contented stretch, he instructed, "Sit up and turn around. Slowly. I'd rather you didn't dump us with that shark swimming over there."

Her heart jumped into her throat. "What shark?"

"Ha. Gotcha."

She slapped his chest. "You're an idiot, and you'll pay for that. Now I hear the *Jaws* theme playing in my head."

Standing up on the board with an easy grace she envied, he scooped up paddle. "So. You want to give it a try this time?"

"Yes," she said on impulse. "I'd like that."

He flashed one of his brilliant grins and held out a hand to help her up. The board wobbled under her feet, but it was quite a bit easier to stand on it than she would have expected. Jude gave her the paddle and with his hands on her waist, turned her around to face forward. His breath whispered over her ear as he explained the basics of how to move the board, sending shivers down her spine. It took a couple tries to get the hang of it, but then they were sailing smoothly forward. The underused muscles in her arms and torso ached with each pull of the paddle, but it was the delicious kind of ache, warm and heady, much like sex with Jude.

"You got it," he said and nuzzled her earlobe. He still hadn't removed his hands from her waist, and in that moment, with the sun turning to rust and sinking toward the horizon, the wind tangling her hair and his warm, solid weight pressed to her back…in that moment, she hoped he never let go of her.

More foolishness, she told herself and concentrated on making the board go straight.

Jude Wilde didn't hang on to anything for long.

Chapter Nineteen

Jude was in an excellent mood. A day of playing tourist, soaking in the sun and natural beauty of the Keys, followed by sex...

Oh, man, the sex. The off-the-charts-hot sex.

It was all exactly what he'd needed and he suspected, what Libby had needed, too—although he bet she'd never admit it.

He smiled to himself and spared a glance for her, sound asleep in the passenger seat, her cheek pillowed in her hand against the window. Her hair had frizzed from their swim and the soaking they got from an evening storm as they raced across the marina parking lot for their car. He resisted the urge to reach over and soothe down the sun-kissed locks. Made himself focus on the road, but found his hand wandering from the steering wheel to rest on her thigh. She stirred but didn't wake, and he smiled again.

Now the rain tap-danced on the roof of the convertible

and lightning zigzagged in the distance over the ocean as the car sailed the Overseas Highway toward home.

Jude felt better than he had in days. Sure, his back was sunburned all to hell—damn Libby for being right about the sunscreen—but even that discomfort couldn't put a damper on his mood.

Damn near perfect day.

He couldn't remember the last time he felt this light, this free. He could become addicted to this. To her. Maybe he already was.

Unable to resist, he sneaked another peek her way. Deep in sleep, she looked completely at peace—no worry lines etched into her forehead, no trace of the sour grapes pinched expression around her mouth. She needed to sleep more, work less, and play more, he decided and then snorted as he imagined her response to that suggestion. But someone had to apply the brakes on the race car that was Elizabeth Pruitt or she was going to burn out her engine. After this was all over, he'd talk her into a worry-free day like today at least once a week. She carried way too much stress and—

Whoa. What? After this was over? Goddammit, he was an idiot for even considering an "after" with her. No chance. Hadn't she told him as much the night she started their affair?

It was sex. No emotions. No strings attached. No after. And he'd gone along with it because he was just desperate enough to be with her that he'd take her any way he could. Except an affair had never been what he wanted when it came to Libby. He'd loved her and had wanted the whole package the night he proposed eight years ago. Libby in a white dress, vowing to stay with him forever. Her pregnant with his two-point-five children. The quaint house with the white picket fence, dog, and minivan.

Loved? No, he was lying to himself. Love, present tense. It was still there, strong as ever, just like their ring in his pocket. But he'd be damned before he told her. She wouldn't accept those words from him anyway. He'd hurt her too badly, which had been his goal, and he'd done a bang-up job of it. Hurt her to protect her. Wasn't he just noble as fuck?

Uh-uh. And after this was over, she would go back to her life and he to his. That would be the end of it. He just wasn't sure if he'd be able to glue the pieces of his life back together again once she was gone.

Far less cheerful than he had been moments before, he lifted his hand off her thigh and focused all of his concentration on the road. Headlights hit his rearview mirror with the blinding force of laser beams. Where the fuck had this car come from? They were on a two-lane road out in the middle of the ocean with no on- or off-ramps. Unless the driver had been going at least twenty above the speed limit—and who would risk that in this rain?—then that car had been following them from the get-go. A chill of awareness shot through Jude's blood, and he fumbled in the center console for his phone.

Libby lifted her head, rubbed at the back of her neck, and squinted out the windshield. "Wow, it's really raining now." Yawning, she looked over at him. "What are you doing?"

"Find my phone. It's in there somewhere."

She twisted in her seat and dug through the compartment with maddening care.

"Faster."

"What's your hurry?"

He forced himself to keep his gaze on the road ahead of him. "I need to check my messages."

"Ugh. Impatient, much? Hang on." More digging around. "Here. Found it." She swiped at the screen with her thumb. "You have a missed call from someone with the initials W.S."

"Wilde Security. My brothers." Another glance in the rearview showed the car had backed off a bit, but was still riding too damn close. "Get into the voice mail." He told her his access code and waited, palm held out for the phone. She never handed it over.

"Oh my God. Jude, listen." Her hand shook as she lowered the phone from her ear and pressed the speaker button. Greer's voice came on the line, booming in the small car.

"…and Cam's source claims K-Bar hasn't been seen in a couple days. We have to assume he's found you, and he's headed your way. Call me as soon as you get this, and we'll come up with an exfil plan to get you two the hell out of there. Take every precaution and don't let Libby out of your sight."

"Oh my God," Libby said again. "Are you going to call him?"

Jude lifted his eyes to the rearview. Car was still on their ass, too close for comfort on a nearly empty road in a torrential downpour. He shook his head. "No. If we move you, he'll just find you again. The safest place for you is Seth's house. We just have to lose him before we get there."

"*What?*"

He tilted his head toward the car. "Behind us. Pretty sure he was tailing us with his headlights off until the rain got too heavy to see the road without them. Hang on. We gotta get to civilization before him. It's our only shot."

As he floored the gas, Libby folded her arms around herself. "This can't be happening."

"It may be nothing," he reminded her. "I may just be a paranoid bastard, and if that's the case, we can laugh about it later. I have trouble believing K-Bar got around all of my brothers' security measures and found you, but I'm not taking any more chances."

A fter abandoning the car with a valet at a busy hotel, she and Jude nipped through the lobby, took a side exit, and made a mad dash through parking lots and private yards until they reached a street teeming with tourists who weren't the least bit daunted by the now-light drizzle of rain. Music floated from the bars lining the street—everything from the mellow tones of an acoustic solo artist to bands blasting covers of popular songs. Chickens pecked along the sidewalk, as undaunted by the crowd as the crowd was by the rain. Jude pulled her past a colorfully dressed busker sitting on the street corner strumming a guitar and playing a tambourine with his foot. Both the man and the old hound sitting patiently at his side wore sunglasses and pirate hats.

Key West. This place was something else.

They slipped into a cozy shop, and Jude hustled her past shelves stuffed with seashell trinkets, snow globes, and cheap jewelry. He grabbed things off the racks as he went, then yanked her into a curtained dressing room. Spinning her toward him, he hiked her shirt over her head before she realized what he was doing.

"Jude, what the hell? We're being followed! We don't have time to screw around in a dressing room."

"Interesting idea for another time," he said. "But right now, you need to change." Using his teeth, he broke the tag off a colorful sarong-like dress and shoved it at her, then quickly shed his own wet clothes. Paying no attention to his nakedness, he ripped off the tags on a pair of khaki shorts and a T-shirt that featured a beer bottle sitting under a palm tree and declared "I Heart Key West, Florida" in green letters.

"C'mon, Libs. Hurry." With that, he dressed and left the fitting room with the price tags in hand. She peeked out, saw him snag a baseball cap and a big floppy hat, his eyes always scanning the windows at the front of the shop, studying the passing crowd on Duval Street. He set the ball cap on his head and smiled charmingly at the cashier as he paid. When he returned a few minutes later, he carried a plastic bag labeled with the shop's name and started stuffing his wet clothes into it.

"Libby, move. Let's go."

She changed into the dress and donned the floppy hat he handed her, then stuffed her own wadded clothes into the bag. "Now what?"

"We're James and Liza Wilson, honeymooners out for a night on Duval Street. Nothing more."

"But what about K-Bar? If he—"

"I'm about 98.9 percent sure we lost him before we ditched the car, but we're gonna stay out, mix in with the crowd for a bit, take a cab to the other side of the island, then hoof it to Seth's. It's going to be a long night."

Numbly, she nodded.

He caught her head in his hands, made her meet his gaze. "I know this place better than I know D.C. He doesn't. We have the advantage."

"I just want to go back to the pool and the cat and your laundry all over the floor. I want to be safe."

"I know." With more tenderness than she thought he possessed, he brushed his lips across her forehead. "I know, babe. And we will, but I have to make sure the house stays safe first, okay?" His hands dropped to her shoulders, rubbed. "You can do this, Libby. You're a strong, smart, independent woman."

"I don't feel like it. I'm scared." It seemed like she'd been scared forever, ever since she received the first doll, but this was the first time she'd allowed herself to admit it to anyone. "I really am. Terrified."

"It's foolish not to be."

"You're not."

"Like hell I'm not." He dazzled her with one of his grins. "I'm just damn good at playing pretend. Now let me see the blushing bride, Liza Wilson. What does she do?"

Libby drew in a breath, straightened her shoulders. "Teacher," she decided.

"Yeah? What grade?"

"Kindergarten."

"Sounds like a headache."

"No, it's fun. She loves—No, wait." Cursing under her breath, she corrected herself with as much conviction in her tone as she could muster, "*I* love it."

"Perfect," Jude said. "And what about James?"

"He's...." She thought about it, then smiled evilly up at him. "An accountant."

"Now that's just cruel. And c'mon, who would believe I spend my days crunching numbers?" With a hand on her lower back, he guided her out of the dressing room. He waved at the cashier as they exited the store. "What about a shark wrangler?"

Okay. Time to get into character for real. Forcing herself not to study every face in the crowd, she slid and arm around his waist. "My dear husband, the only shark you can wrangle is the plastic one in our pool."

"Hey." He stopped, whirled her around, and fitted her against his body. "I wrangled you, didn't I?" As his lips dipped down to brush hers, he added in a whisper, "You're talking way too loud and sound like you're reciting a script. Just relax, babe. Pretend we don't have anyone after us, and I'm someone you actually love."

Her stomach sank into her toes. Someone she loved. Oh, yeah, like that was going to be hard, considering the only man she'd ever loved besides her father stood in front of her with his arms tightly around her and concern in his pale blue eyes.

"Okay." She swallowed down the lump rising in her throat and offered a weak smile. "I can do that. I'll just picture Robert Downey Jr."

And like that the worry vanished and his eyes narrowed as a scowl creased his forehead. "You *love* Robert Downey Jr.?"

"Who doesn't?"

Grumbling under his breath, Jude clasped her hand and guided her into the nighttime party crowd on Duval Street.

Chapter Twenty

Jude waited until Libby excused herself to bed before making the call to his brothers. Even after he peeked in on her and found her curled on her side in the big bed, sound asleep, he still puttered around for another half hour before grabbing his cell phone and stepping out onto the patio. Part of that hesitation was because he didn't want to scare her more by talking about the nitty-gritty of the mission in front of her. Mostly, he was just putting it off because he knew Reece was going to hit the roof.

Fun, fun.

It was nearly a quarter past one in the morning, but he'd try the office phone first. Reece didn't have any kind of life, but even if he was at home, he'd have the office cell with him. Greer didn't trust landlines so all business was conducted on burner phones.

The earlier rain had washed away the humidity in the air, leaving the night clear and cool. For once, all was quiet.

He knew the party on Duval Street was probably just now swinging into high gear, but this end of town had called it a night early. No music came from the beach, not even the lone guitar that often strummed through the night until the first rays of morning spread over the ocean.

Jude stayed underneath the portico, sat in one of the wicker chairs, and stared at his phone. Pruitt's lawyer had left three voice mails. He ignored them, but then scrolled blindly through his missed call list, stalling for time. Man, he really didn't want to make this call.

The *pat-pat-pat* of soft paws caught his attention, and he lifted his gaze to see Sam had followed him outside. The big cat stopped in front of him, blinked its green eyes, twitched its tail, and in one mighty leap, landed gracefully on his lap.

"Damn cat," Jude grumbled, but then heard the rhythmic purr pumping from the animal's throat, and his heart melted just a bit. So maybe he could forgive the beast for scratching Libby all to hell.

Sam rubbed against his hand still holding the cell phone, almost as if assuring him it would all be okay. He sighed in surrender and scratched the cat's white chin. "All right, Fuzz Butt. You're cute. Sorta. But don't tell Libby I said that. She'd have way too much fun I-told-ya-so-ing me."

Purring like an outboard motor, Sam walked in a circle, plopped down on Jude's lap, shot a leg into the air, and proceeded to lick his balls. Or the spot where his balls should have been. Poor animal had been snipped. Jude winced and resisted to urge to reach between his own legs to protect his equipment.

"Yeah, you won major sympathy points there, pal." He rubbed a hand down the cat's back, then gave him a light push. "Now get gone. Go cuddle up to Libby. She needs it, and I have a phone call to make."

As if Sam understood, he jumped down and trotted into the house, still purring. Jude watched until the cat disappeared from sight, then turned his gaze back to the phone. Started to dial. Stopped. Tossed the phone from hand to hand.

"Goddammit."

He hit speed dial before he could talk himself out of it. It rang twice—once more than usual—and to his surprise, Camden answered, sounding as if he hadn't been to bed yet.

"You got Greer's message?" he asked.

The tension seeped out of Jude like water from a sieve. Cam, he could talk to easily without the conversation devolving into a shouting match. "About K-Bar's disappearance? Yeah. Where did that intel come from?"

"One of my informants," Cam said and bit into something with a loud crunch. Probably one of the carrot sticks he'd taken to eating like candy after he quit smoking last year. "Soup's reliable. Strung out, but his info's always solid. He says K-Bar wouldn't skip because Mama K-Bar put up her house for bond and her son wouldn't want her ending up homeless. I believe him."

"So where does that leave us?"

"I spent my day casting a net. If he shows anywhere in the city, we'll be the first to know."

"He may not be in the city," Jude said and told Cam about the car that had been tailing them tonight. His brother reacted about like expected, with a litany of ear-blistering and creative curses.

He waited until Cam took a breath and added, "Which

is why I need Reece to work his computer magic and lay a virtual trail to anywhere other than Key West."

"Not happening. Reece is out," Camden said. A tab popped on a can in the background. A beer, no doubt. Man, Jude could use one himself.

"What do you mean, out?"

"He took a home security contract that came in yesterday."

"Fuck." He dragged his hand through his hair and rubbed the back of his neck. Sighed. Really, he didn't know why he was surprised. "The last time we spoke, he wasn't happy with me."

"So what else is new?"

"But I never thought he'd actually leave me hanging."

"You did almost blow the mission wide open. You endangered Libby Pruitt's life."

"No, I didn't."

"I'm sorry," Cam said, sounding not the least bit apologetic. Actually, there was a thick undercurrent of pissed off in his voice. "I have to side with Reece on this one. You were careless."

"C'mon! There was no real threat in anyone seeing that Internet video and linking me to Libby. Not unless they wanted to dig back eight years and even then, it would be a difficult connection to make. I already told you I was careful about who saw us together."

Camden made a sound full of disgust. "Man, you know I love you, but you are a complete asshole. Mom would be ashamed, the way you go through women like other men go through socks."

Jude hissed softly as the barb struck home. Okay, that hurt, especially coming from Cam. He expected—hell, even looked forward to—those kind of remarks from Reece. But not Cam, the Wilde family's glue, the peacemaker, the only one of his brothers that understood him. Or so he thought.

"Well," he finally managed. At least his voice didn't sound as raw as his emotions felt. "Everyone has flaws."

"Some people more than others. You're thirty fucking years old, Jude. When are you gonna straighten up your life?" Before he could formulate a response, Cam muttered a curse. "Sorry, I didn't mean that. I'm exhausted, and my mouth's working faster than my brain. I'm starting to sound like Reece."

"No. You're right. You're both right. When this is over…" He trailed off. He didn't know what would happen, but something had to change. He was tired of pretending. Tired of wearing a smile while everything else stayed locked up in his chest, slowly clawing him into shreds from the inside out.

"It is over," Cam said. "Greer wants to pull you both out and relocate Libby to her father's cabin in Vermont."

So Pruitt had talked Greer into the cabin idea. If Jude thought that would do any good, he'd be in packing their bags now—wait. Cam only mentioned Libby's name. Relocate *Libby*. "What about me?"

Cam stayed silent for a moment. "You're coming home. Pruitt wants me to stay with her."

"No."

"Jude—"

"No fucking way."

A pause. "Goddammit. Are you sleeping with her again?"

Okay, he hadn't meant to give himself away like that. "So what?"

"So you're seriously going to risk her life for a few more

nights of fun?"

Jude's teeth ground together so hard he felt his jaw pop from the pressure. "I'd *never* risk her life. For anything."

More silence. Then, "Whoa. You care about her."

"And you call yourself a detective? That should have been obvious from the start."

"Yeah, I knew you cared—*at one time*. But I had no idea you're still in l—"

"We're not leaving," Jude interrupted. "There's nowhere safer for her than Seth's house. This place is a fortress. Top of the line security, better than anything we have in our arsenal of tricks. Can't Vaughn lay the cyber trail back to D.C. or even to the cabin in Vermont? Make it look like we left?"

Cam exhaled hard. "Vaughn's good, but he's not Reece. If K-Bar, or whoever, had the technology to track you to Key West in the first place, there's a good chance he'll see through it. I still think you should exfil. Greer's gonna have a fit that you're refusing."

No doubt about it, and Jude was extremely glad he wouldn't be around to receive the brunt of Greer's temper this time. "Believe me, Cam, I want her safe as much as any-one. If I didn't think she was safe here anymore, I'd be the first to say so, but there's no place on Earth better to hide than in this house. You know how paranoid Seth got after everything he went through."

"Then you need to utilize every safety measure he has in place," Cam said. "We lay that trail, you'll have to stay inside the house. No more jaunts to the beach in your underwear. No more paddle boarding trips. No Duval Street. No grocery shopping. Everything will be delivered to the front door by men I'll personally pick. You're not even walking out to the curb for the newspaper, got me?"

Jude thought back on the day. So perfect in every way until he spotted that car tailing them and now Libby would never remember anything but the fear of running from someone who may not have even been chasing them. This threat to her was a boogeyman—intangible, but scary enough to make you check under the bed twice before going to sleep.

And, like he'd told her in the car, he was done taking chances.

"Yeah, I got you. We'll stay inside the gate," he said to Cam. "Call me as soon as you find out where the hell K-Bar's hiding."

Libby heard the patio door slide shut and stilled her hand on Sam's back, feigning sleep. Jude's footfalls came softly as he extinguished lights on the way to the bedroom, but he hesitated in the doorway, and she lifted one eyelid to watch him. He stood just inside the room, a pool of cool moonlight splashing around his feet from the sliding glass doors that led to the garden and pool. Simply standing there, staring at the bed. She felt his eyes sweep over her and despite the chill in the air, her skin heated in response with the memory of sun, water, and sex.

He finally moved around the end of the bed, stripping off his clothes and dropping them on the floor, kicking them out of the way when they landed in his path. She should tell him to pick them up and put them away like a normal adult, but she said nothing. There would be time for that tomorrow.

He slid underneath the covers and spooned up behind

her. She should tell him to go back to the couch and leave her alone, but the idea of sleeping in this big bed alone tonight sent icy snakes of fear slithering down her spine. She didn't want to be alone. All right, if she was perfectly honest with herself, it was more than a need for companionship. Not just anyone would do. It was all him. She didn't want to be without him, specifically, tonight.

So instead of telling him off like she knew she should, she reveled in his tattooed arms encasing her in their strength, relaxed in the comfort of his long frame pressed chest-to-back against her, drifted in the tenderness of the moment as he buried his face in her hair.

"I will keep you safe," he whispered.

She turned to him in the dark, unable to fake sleep any longer. She clasped his face between her palms and kissed him, a light back and forth brush of her lips across his. "I know."

Chapter Twenty-One

The first week of July, a hurricane churning out near Cuba made the weather turn. Gone were the warm, sun-drenched spring days, replaced with muggy, overcast, and rainy afternoons that seemed endless. Jude was lucky if he got his swim in, but the punishing exercises he'd been putting himself through in the gym were no longer taking the edge off his restlessness and the lack of outside stimulation made him twitchy.

The weather took its toll on Libby, too. With each passing day, she seemed more morose, talking to him, joking with him, less and less. He tried to give her some space, but when he walked into the house from tinkering with Seth's car in the garage and found her sitting on the couch with tears rolling down her face as she watched TV, that was the final straw. He set aside the rag he'd been wiping his greasy hands on and knelt down in front of her.

"Libs, what's wrong?"

She sniffled and swiped away the tears with the fingers of one hand. "Nothing."

"Yeah, I cry over nothing all the time."

That got him a little smile as he'd hoped it would. "It's stupid."

"I'm good with stupid."

She motioned to the TV with the remote in her hand. On screen, a hot dog commercial showed a happy-happy family passing heaping dishes of food around a packed picnic table. Jude watched until the commercial cut to the next, an advertisement for the local news talking about the possibility of cancelling tomorrow's firework show.

"Tomorrow's the Fourth of July," she said and brushed away another tear. "I've never missed one with my family, but now I'm stuck here, and I won't get to see my parents or any of my aunts, uncles, cousins. My grandparents. I miss them. I won't be home to celebrate with them."

Christ, he was a nitwit. Of course she'd been upset—it was a holiday, and she was homesick. Why hadn't that occurred to him before now?

Holidays had been no big deal in the Wilde family since his parents died. Actually, this was the first year all of his brothers were in the same country for the holiday. Someone had always been overseas, and whoever else was available might get together in a bar for a beer or two, but that was the extent of it. He couldn't remember having a real family dinner since he was nine...but he suddenly wanted one. With Libby.

He leaned in and gave her a light kiss. "This will be over soon enough. Once my brothers find K-Bar, he's going back to prison for breaking his parole, and you'll be safe to go home and see your folks."

But until then, he had some plans to make.

Libby woke later than usual the next morning and lay in bed, staring up at the ceiling fan for a long time, debating whether she should get up. She turned her head on the pillow and looked at the alarm clock. Nearly noon. Really, what was the point? She could hear rain drumming against the roof, so it wasn't as if she could go outside and soak in some sun.

Boy, she missed the sun.

But she missed her family even more.

"Ugh. Can someone say pity party?" Disgusted with herself, she shoved off the blankets and headed toward the bathroom for a shower. So she was missing her family's barbeque tonight. At least doing so ensured that she'd be around for next year's festivities. Better to spend one holiday lonely than spend the rest of her holidays in a grave.

She showered quickly, wrestled her damp hair into a ponytail, and tossed on an oversize T-shirt and cotton shorts. No sense in putting on anything else. She wasn't going any—

Stepping into the hallway, she stopped in surprise at the delicious scents from the kitchen. Jude stood at the counter, reading the directions on the back of a refrigerated piecrust tin. He was in his favorite basketball shorts, shirtless, his back turned toward her, and that old curiosity about his tattoo pulled her forward. Dammit, why'd she leave her glasses in the bedroom?

Just as she got close enough to make out some of the

words on his spine, he turned and grinned. "You're awake."

Pretending she hadn't been trying to read his tattoo again, she casually moved to his side to examine the ingredients he had spread on the counter. "And you're…baking?"

"Just another of my skills. It's a long and varied list."

"Which is why you're using canned apple filling and a refrigerated crust, I'm sure."

"Hey now. I'm working with what I have. It wasn't easy to put this much together on short notice. I now owe Camden's cop buddy a favor, which, between you and me, freaks me the hell out."

She laughed and dipped her finger into the pre-made apple filling. Not bad. "Seriously, though, what are you doing?"

His smile faded, and he focused on pressing the crust into a pie plate. "You were so upset yesterday. I figured you couldn't be at your family's Fourth of July, so I'd make one for you here. I even got you sparklers."

Libby stared at him. It wasn't until he lifted a hand and pressed her jaw closed that she realized her mouth had been hanging open. She scanned the counter again. All of the fixings for a barbeque sat there in a line.

"Jude…" Flustered, she didn't know what else to say.

"Is it okay?" he asked. "My brothers and I don't do holidays, so I wasn't entirely sure—I mean, I know it's not home, but I just thought—"

Libby stood on her toes, cutting off his rambles with a kiss. "It's perfect. Thank you."

His grin returned, and he dabbed flour on her chin. "Wanna help?"

"You bet your ass I do. I have been so incredibly bored this week."

"Oh good. I thought I was the only one."

They ate dinner a little before five, and it was actually quite good for a last-minute, cobbled-together meal. The fact that Jude had even thought to do this for her made everything taste that much better.

She shoved away her half-eaten second slice of pie and sat back. Jude smiled across the table at her. "Eyes bigger than your stomach?"

"Waaay bigger."

He pulled the plate toward him and cut off a piece. "Mind?"

"No." She scowled as he made short work of the rest of the pie. "I can't believe you're still eating. Where do you put it all?"

"Mm. I could tell you…" He pointed his fork at her. "But then I'd have to eat you, too. Actually, that might not be a bad idea. Like dessert. I love the way you squeak when I go down on—"

"Be good, Jude. We're at the dinner table." She laughed when he grinned unapologetically and waggled his brows.

"You know, we haven't done it on a table yet."

"The pool table counts."

"No, it doesn't."

"You're nuts."

"Yeah, I am. Thanks for noticing." Finishing off the final bite of pie, he licked his fork clean, and then began gathering their plates. "Dining table. I'll have to keep it in mind for another time, but right now I'm so full the only thing I want to do with you is nap."

"I'm so on board with that idea." But, wow, moving anywhere seemed like a chore. "Except you'll have to carry me to the bedroom."

From the kitchen behind her, he gave a *yeah right* snort.

"So is that a no?"

Jude didn't answer. In fact, she didn't hear anything from him, no shuffling, no water running over their dishes in the sink. She started to turn to see what he was up to now and found him standing beside her, a cell phone shoved toward her face. She blinked when he dropped it into her hand. It appeared to be midcall, the timer on the screen ticking off seconds as she frowned at it, then up at him.

"What's this?"

He simply nodded and motioned for her to lift it to her ear.

Confused, she did so and—

At the sound of her mother's voice on the other end of the line, instant tears blurred her vision. "Mom?"

Oh God. Her parents. He'd called her parents!

Eyes wide, she stared at him in shock. The nerve of the man, standing there grinning like a maniac, all proud of himself for breaking his own rules. She wanted to throw herself into his arms and hug him. The nerve.

And also the heart.

God, he had so much heart it was a wonder it all fit inside his chest.

Libby turned her focus to her mother's excited chattering. After a few minutes, her father came on the line, less excited but definitely happy to talk to her. Although, as usual, he tried to hide it under a gruff facade. In deference to her safety, it was a short conversation and saying good-bye to them was the hardest thing she'd ever done, but when she hung up the phone, all of the sadness that had been weighing her down this past week had vanished.

Phone still in hand, she turned in her chair and watched Jude as he scrubbed at a stubborn pan in the sink. His jeans hung low on his hips, and he'd taken off the shirt he'd donned before dinner, probably to keep it from getting wet. His muscles flexed with the work, making his tattoo dance along his spine.

Slowly, Libby stood and crossed the kitchen to his side. She touched his arm. "Can please I see it? Your tattoo?"

Exhaling hard, he looked over at her, held her gaze for a long moment.

"Are you ashamed of it?" She couldn't think of another reason why he'd be so sensitive about it.

"No. Never." For some reason, his gaze dropped to the cell phone still in her hand, and he stared at it like it was going to give him answers to all of life's hardest questions. Finally, he shrugged, dried off his hands on a towel, and gave her his back. Her fingers itched to touch him, but she feared he'd shy away and she'd never find out what his tattoo said. She kept her hands to herself and read the words he'd thought important enough to ink permanently into his skin.

Meredith, my love…

She jerked backward in shock. A love letter. He had tattooed a *love letter* to his spine. Her throat worked, but for a long moment, she couldn't produce any sound around the surge of pain that froze her vocal chords.

"Who's Meredith?" she finally choked.

"My mother."

All the air left her lungs in a burst that was too close to a relieved sob for comfort. "Your mother." She reached out with trembling fingers and traced the outline of the ballet slippers hanging from one side of the broken angel wings. It was so obvious that she wondered why she hadn't she made the connection sooner. His mother was a dancer. And the dog tags on the other half of the wings? His father had been career Army.

A memorial to the parents he'd loved and lost far too soon.

"The words—" He stopped, cleared his throat. "My father wrote them. His wedding vow to her."

"Jude," she breathed and circled around to face him, but he was staring at the floor. She always accused him of being childish, all that time never forgetting that he was very much a man. But in this moment, he looked so much like the vulnerable child he must have once been, and she wanted nothing more than to hold him close. Comfort him. She touched his cheek and miserable blue eyes lifted, met hers, clung.

"Do you want to tell me about them?"

He shook his head.

How absurd to feel disappointed. He was obviously wrestling with a personal demon that she had no right to help him slay. His problem. His life. It shouldn't matter to her. She'd spent eight years convincing herself it didn't matter—that *he* didn't matter. And look how that turned out. It took only three weeks with him to negate those eight years.

Despite it all, she still loved him. Had never stopped, probably never would—and she could never tell him. The only thing permanent in Jude Wilde's life were those tattoos. Hanging on to him would be like trying to hang on to a hummingbird as it darted from flower to flower. Unfair to them both.

On impulse, she set the cell phone on the counter and wound her arms around his waist, laid her cheek against his chest, and held him. Maybe it could only be for the space of a heartbeat, but she held on and let herself enjoy it. He returned her embrace hard, and his whole being seemed to shudder. Whether from relief or something else, she didn't dare guess.

"I sneaked out that night," he murmured into her hair. "The night my parents died."

She squeezed him tighter, but kept her mouth shut. It surprised her that he'd confided even that much, and she didn't want to seem like she was pressuring him.

"I wanted nothing more than see *Jurassic Park*," he continued after a seemingly endless moment of silence. "I begged them all summer to take me to the theater, but they wouldn't. Mom said it wasn't a movie for a ten-year-old. Hell, she wouldn't even let Reece watch it, and he was thirteen. It seemed so important to me at the time. So important.

"One of my friends got it on video for his birthday, and a group of us planned to sneak over to his house later that night to watch it. I'd seen Greer sneak out enough times to know exactly how it was done, so off I went in my dinosaur PJs, ready to get the shit scared out of me by T-Rex. I never considered what my parents would think when they came to tuck me in and saw my bed empty, my window open, my shoes and coat still in my closet."

"They thought someone had taken you," she concluded.

"Yeah. They left Greer at home with Reece and the twins and went to the police. They filed a report, then launched their own search, driving up and down the streets, calling my name, looking for any signs of me. By that point, I was already back in my room, sound asleep. Reece found me, tried to get a hold of them to tell them I was all right...but this was '93. Not everyone had cell phones back then."

He stopped. Libby rubbed her cheek against his chest. "What happened to them?"

Jude blew out a long, slow breath. "They stopped at a gas station to fill up before continuing their search and walked right into an armed robbery. The gunman shot Dad in the head as he went inside to pay for the gas. Yanked Mom out of the car and shot her four times. Left her to bleed out in the parking lot and stole the car. She made it to the hospital before—before she died."

Libby blinked back tears and held him tighter, offering the comfort she could. "Did they catch the guy?"

"No, but it didn't matter. There was only one person responsible for their deaths."

"Jude, no—"

"I envy you," he said, cutting off her protest. He motioned to the cell phone. "What you have with your parents. Hell, even the fact that you still have your parents. I envy you. I always have."

Chapter Twenty-Two

Libby opened her mouth, but after that whopper of a confession, one he hadn't meant to make, he couldn't stay to hear whatever pity she was about to lay on him. He strode into the bedroom, needing space from her, but finding the room resonated with her essence. The faint hint of vanilla in the air from her perfume, her nightshirt folded so neatly on the end of the made bed. Even as miserable as he felt, he had to smile. Meticulous even when she'd been feeling blue—she was his opposite in almost every way. In the rare occasions when he got mopey, his apartment usually suffered for it.

Jude sat on the edge of the bed and cradled his head in his hands. Part of him wanted to hate Libby for dragging him through the muck of the past. He never let himself think about that night but, he supposed, he'd never managed to leave it behind him, either. It colored everything he'd ever done in his life. And, hell, to this day he couldn't watch

Jurassic Park without bawling like a baby.

Maybe it was time to face it.

The door opened a crack, and Libby peeked into the dim room, the light from the hallway creating a halo effect around her golden hair. After a moment of indecision, she came inside, shut the door, and moved to stand in front of him.

"I'm sorry," she whispered.

Fuck. Who knew two little words could pack such a punch? Appalled that his vision had gone blurry, he snaked a hand around her waist and pulled her toward him, burying his face in the soft fabric of her T-shirt over her belly.

"I shouldn't have asked." Her fingers sifted through his hair, trailed down the back of his neck and spine. Pleasurable goose bumps swept over his skin.

Her name left his lips on a groan, and as he tilted his face up, her lips descended on his. He parted his knees, inviting her to step into him, wanting her closer, needing her closer. Funny how just a moment ago, he'd thought he needed some time alone, but he'd been so ridiculously wrong about that. He didn't need space. All he needed was her. He had a sinking feeling that she was all he'd ever need. She was definitely all he'd ever wanted, but he'd learned long ago that yearning for something he would never be able to have was pointless. All they had was this fling. This night. Possibly tomorrow night, but that was no guarantee. His brothers could capture K-Bar at any moment, and then this would all be over. He had to take what he could get now.

No emotions.

He could do that. He'd done it most of his life.

As their mouths fused together in a slow burn of passion,

his hands dipped under her shirt and caressed the skin of her back. She sighed into his mouth, then pulled away long enough to whisk her shirt over her head. Standing, he unbuttoned his jeans, but couldn't keep his hands to himself. Undressing her held a lot more appeal anyway, and he skimmed her shorts down her legs, trailing his lips along all the golden skin he found on the way. Her fingers dug into his scalp, and he felt the tug on his hair all the way to the tip of his cock. Man, he loved it when she did that.

No emotions.

In a burst of movement, he cupped her lovely, lace-covered ass, scooped her up until her legs wound around his waist, and switched their positions, laying her gently on the bed. He lowered himself on top of her, loving the way everything soft on her body yielded to everything hard on his. And the way she smiled up at him like she had a secret she was about to divulge. And the way her glasses sat slightly crooked on her nose, knocked askew by him, and how she didn't give a shit.

Jude lifted her glasses off and folded them carefully on the nightstand. Turning her head on the pillow, she reached out to help, but he caught her hand and nuzzled the exposed column of her neck.

No emotions.

A hum of pleasure vibrated her throat under his lips, and his body reacted as if she had zapped him, every nerve ending firing at the same moment. He reclaimed her mouth, and his senses filled to capacity with her taste, her vanilla scent, her soft skin, the sound of her breathing, the beat of her heart…

No emotions?

Yeah, right.

Something was different about Jude tonight. He took his time, drawing every kiss, every caress out until every inch of her skin flushed hot and every breath came out as a sigh or a moan. This wasn't the fast, hard, bed-rocking sex she'd had with him in the past, but something else entirely. Something gentle and pure and genuine.

If she didn't know any better, she'd think he was making love to her.

With a sigh, she opened herself to him, taking him deep into her body—and, she feared, her heart. But she wouldn't say it, wouldn't let herself feel anything but the pleasure of this moment. She shut her eyes, focused only on the sensations of their joining, but he stopped moving, and his fingers trailed along her cheek. He cupped a hand around the back of her neck and lifted her toward him, his lips sealing over hers with such possessiveness that her eyes popped open in surprise. He stared right back at her, every wild, passionate, insane emotion she was trying so hard not to feel reflected in his gaze.

Heart in her throat, she tightened her legs around his hips and pushed herself up with her arms. He relented easily, laying back and letting her take control. His hands slid upward from her waist, released the clasp of her bra, and skimmed the straps off her shoulders. He traced the fullness of each breast as the bra fell away, then smoothed his fingers down her arms until they found her hands. He pressed their palms together, his fingers twice as big and deeply tanned, hers smaller and only a few sun-kissed shades lighter. Smiling slightly, he twined their fingers together. Somehow, that tender joining was even more intimate than the one at their hips, and emotion thickened in her throat.

Did she dare take the risk of loving him again?

Really, did she even have a choice?

She wouldn't think about it. Not tonight. She'd just feel. Enjoy. And pretend he didn't already hold her still-fragile heart in his hands.

Chapter Twenty-Three

Jude half woke to the sound of his phone *bzz-bzz-bzz*ing on the nightstand and slapped at it to shut it up. It stopped. Satisfied, he rolled toward Libby and nuzzled the back of her neck. She gave a contented sigh, but otherwise didn't stir.

They'd wiped each other out last night, making love until he barely had enough energy left to drag the blankets off the floor and cover them before sleep overtook him. He, for one, was one hundred thousand percent okay with that. He wasn't hearing any complaints from her, either, and he thought he might even be ready to do it all over again.

Make love.

That was exactly what they had done last night. It transcended sex and had proved more satisfying—and more exhausting—than anything else he'd ever experienced in a bed. His cock couldn't wait for more and stood at rigid attention, prodding at the cleft of Libby's lovely ass, ready for action as a good soldier should be. But the rest of his body was so not on board, still too physically exhausted to act on the urge. Another hour of zzzs, he told his lower half, and then all bets were off because he definitely needed to be making love to Libby again soon.

He nuzzled his face in the long silk of her unbound hair, inhaled her scent, and drifted toward sleep with a smile — until the phone started ringing again.

"Goddammit." He reached for it and rubbed his eyes before checking the screen. Camden. Grumbling, he answered. "Someone had better be dead."

"Someone is," Camden said, and he sounded exhausted. "K-Bar."

Jude blinked, his mind running sluggishly, still fuzzy with sleep, and he wasn't sure he'd heard that right. "Wait, what?"

"He's dead. As in he's no longer living. Decapitated and hacked into pieces dead."

"Okay, okay, I got it." Wide awake now, Jude glanced over at Libby and told himself to man up as a heaviness centered in his chest. It was over. All of it, including their affair. Goddammit. "Hey, that's great news."

"Not even close," Cam said. "He's been dead a while. At least a week, probably ever since he went missing. There's no way he could have flown to Key West and followed you two."

Slowly, so as not to wake Libby, Jude slid his arm out from underneath her and sat up on the edge of the bed. He kept his voice low. "What happened?"

"Kenneth Burke killed him."

"GQ? Pruitt's lawyer? What makes you think that?"

"The blue car that almost ran you and Libby over? The

pregnant woman it was stolen from lives in the apartment complex behind Burke's condo."

"So he could have known the woman was on bed rest and wouldn't report it missing," Jude said and glanced over at Libby's sleeping form. "That's definitely suspicious, but Libby would ream you a new one for calling that proof of his involvement."

"You haven't heard the worst of it yet," his brother continued. "We wouldn't have realized he was practically the woman's neighbor if he hadn't had the sheer ego to use the car *again* for K-Bar's murder. The woman wised up and had her husband move her bed closer to the window so she could keep an eye on the car, and she saw him take it. Called the cops and described him, but by the time they tracked down the vehicle, K-Bar was dead in the backseat."

"Damn." Squeezing his eyes shut, Jude pinched the bridge of his nose as a tension headache started to throb in the center of his forehead. "Burke's called me nonstop every day. I just thought he was doing it on the colonel's behalf."

"No, Pruitt's been dealing directly with us," Camden said. "The lawyer shouldn't even be involved at this point, but his credit card shows a recent one-day trip to Key West. Best guess is he saw your iguana video online and flew down there to find Libby."

"Does he know our cover identities?"

"He must, otherwise he wouldn't have found you at the boat charter place on Big Pine Key."

"Shit. Where is he now?"

"We don't know."

Jude groaned. "Cam, that's not what I want to hear. Did you search his place?"

"Eva did."

Although Cam's former partner with the Metropolitan PD homicide division was thorough, Jude wished his brothers had conducted the search instead. "What did she find?"

Cam exhaled slowly. "Hundreds of paper dolls and a few pairs of what Eva assumes are Libby's underwear."

A chill scraped across the back of Jude's neck. "Jesus Christ."

"He has notebooks filled with letters to her and hundreds of pictures of her that date back to her law school years. Some she clearly posed for, but she didn't realize she was being photographed in most of them."

Jude reached over and shook Libby awake. She blinked up at him and started to smile, but the look on his face must have been grim because she bolted upright. "What's wrong?"

"Did you know Kenneth Burke in law school?" he asked.

Her forehead wrinkled in confusion, and she fumbled for her glasses. "Yes. We hung out with the same people. Why?"

"Is he the guy you slept with?"

She wrapped her arms around herself as color filled her cheeks. "No, but I don't see how that's relevant to anything."

"Did he ever show any sexual interest in you?"

She squirmed, obviously uneasy, but he couldn't mince words to make his questions more comfortable. Not when he felt this niggling sensation of urgency.

"We went on one date my first semester of law school," she answered at last. "I thought it was time to move on, and I chose him because he's your opposite in almost every way. During dinner, we both realized there wasn't anything romantic between us, and that was the end of it. We've been friends since."

Uh-huh, Jude thought. More like she placed Burke in the friend category and he'd gone along with it to stay close to her. But somewhere along the way, his interest had become a very dangerous obsession.

The front gate buzzer sounded. Once. Twice. Three times. Four, five, six…nine times in total.

Libby started at the sound. "What's that?"

"Shit," Jude said into the phone and shot off the bed, grabbing his weapon from the bedside table. "Cam, someone's at the gate."

His brother echoed his curse. "Don't answer it. Get Libby somewhere safe."

"Call me some fucking backup." He hung up and yanked on his basketball shorts, and then he scooped Libby into his arms, bedsheet and all, and carried her into the closet. She didn't protest like he thought she would. She merely wrapped her arms around his neck and held on as he punched a code on a panel in the back wall.

A hidden door swooshed open with a slight breeze due to the pressure-lock, and he stepped into the twelve-by-twelve room that used to be a second bedroom. Now it rivaled any doomsday prepper's bunker, which was one of the reasons he'd been so determined to keep Libby in this house. He had no doubt this room would survive a nuclear blast, and Seth kept it stocked with several years' worth of supplies, including all kinds of weapons, some of which he probably shouldn't legally own.

Jude set Libby down and studied the wall of monitors that covered every inch of the house and property. Kenneth

Burke stood at the gate with Colonel Pruitt directly in front of him, both of them soaked by the drizzle of rain. Pruitt looked up and down the street, then reached out and leaned on the buzzer again. Nine times.

Short, short, short. Long, long, long. Short, short, short.

S.O.S. in Morse code.

Jude hit the switch for the intercom. "I'm not opening the gate, Pruitt."

"Good. Don't. Burke is the stalker. He tricked me into bringing him here, told me she was in danger," Pruitt said as if giving a sitrep, and the lawyer's eyes rounded in surprise.

And there it was—the gun. Burke raised it to Pruitt's temple, pressed it so hard into his flesh that the colonel couldn't hide his wince.

"Then you'll kill him," Burke said. "Are you ready to watch him die?"

"You won't," Jude said, even though he didn't believe his own words. If Burke was demented enough to decapitate K-Bar, the man would have no problem killing Pruitt. But he had to keep Burke talking just long enough for the cavalry to arrive. "Run a man over with a car? Sure, I can see that, but—"

"That was a warning," Burke said. "I tried telling Libby to watch out for you."

Watch out. The message on the windshield of her car. Jude cursed at himself. He'd been so focused on it as a threat, it never occurred to him that it might be a warning instead.

"But then she kissed you," Burke continued. "I have been waiting *years* for her to realize how right we are together, giving her little gifts, little nudges. Then you come along out of the blue, and it was like our relationship meant nothing to her. Nothing. Understandably, I lost my mind for a moment, thought maybe I could scare you away from her so she'd come to her senses."

"It takes more than Ford Taurus to scare me, asshole."

Libby came up to stand beside him and touched his arm with trembling fingers, her complexion as white as the sheet he'd wrapped her in. "W-what's going on?"

He tried to block the monitors. "It's all under control—"

"Is that my dad?" Her hand covered a gasp. "And Kenneth?"

"Libby," Burke called, his voice going all sickly sweet. On screen, his features softened. "I know you can hear me. Let me in, sweetheart."

"Kenneth?" she repeated faintly. She closed her eyes, and her skin took on a sickly green cast. "Oh God."

"Libby, open the gate, or I'll kill him."

Jude wrapped his arms around her shivering frame and pressed his lips to her temple. "Don't listen to him. Cam's sending help. We just have to hold him off until the police get here."

"Oh, yes, I'll kill your father," Burke said matter-of-factly. "I won't like it, but I'll do it, and then his blood will be on your hands, sweetheart. Can you live with that? I don't think so."

Libby lunged for the intercom. "Kenneth, please, don't hurt him. We're opening the gate now. Please, don't hurt my dad."

Jude caught her hand before she found the button for the gate's lock. She stared up at him, her eyes huge and shining with terror behind her glasses, a plea in her gaze.

"Jude," she said around a sob. "He's my father."

"It's my job to keep you safe."

"Wouldn't you have done anything to keep your father alive? Even if it meant risking your own life?"

"Yes," he said without flinching. "But I can't let you. I—" *Love you*. The words caught. He'd never said those words to her or anyone else. Since his parents died, they were just too damn hard to articulate. "I can't put you in danger."

She cupped his cheek in her palm, and he leaned into it, pressing his hand over hers.

"You're not putting me in danger," she said softly. "I am." Before he could stop her, she slammed her free hand down on the gate release.

Swearing, Jude spun toward the monitors. On screen, Burke nudged Pruitt through the gate with the gun's muzzle. Fuck, fuck, fuck. He grasped Libby by the shoulders. "You need to stay here in this room no matter what, you understand? You get my cell phone out of the bedroom, then stay in here and call the police. I'll stall him as long as I can."

"My dad—"

"Is well trained. He can handle himself." He kissed her hard. "If you leave this room, you'll just give Burke what he wants—an extra target."

She nodded and swallowed hard. "I'll stay. I promise."

Somehow, he doubted that. He pulled her in for another quick kiss, silently pleading with her to keep that promise and wishing like hell Seth was here. That bastard Burke would already be dead with a capital D, and Libby would be safe. When Seth got behind the scope of a sniper rifle, he didn't miss. One shot, one kill—a skill Jude didn't have that would definitely come in handy right about now.

Libby caught his hand before he turned away and

motioned to the glass-fronted gunroom that, he remembered, used to be a walk-in closet. "You should take a gun."

He shook his head, offered a reassuring smile. Without Seth's sharpshooter skills, a weapon would only exacerbate the problem, and he knew other ways to kill besides with a gun. "I'll be fine." He winked. "Trust me, I've done this before."

She laughed, but it came out more like a sob. "If you get killed, I'm going to be very pissed off."

"Babe, c'mon, give me some credit here. I wouldn't dare deny you the pleasure of killing me yourself."

This time, when she laughed, it sounded more authentic. "It's amazing you've lived this long."

"So Camden always tells me." He paused in the doorway, glanced back. There she stood wrapped in a sheet, her hair falling a tangled mess around her shoulders, her glasses slightly askew. His heart squeezed so hard it hurt. "Now go get my phone and some clothes and lock yourself in this room. Tell the cops what's happening and open the gate when they get here. This will all be over soon."

He didn't wait for a reply but hurried out through the bedroom, careful to shut the door behind him. He emerged into the living room as the front door opened, and Pruitt stepped in, followed closely by Burke with the gun still pressed against the colonel's back.

Kenneth fucking Burke.

Shit, he really hadn't seen this coming. He'd pegged the guy as a pretentious yuppie but hadn't thought him capable of stalking and murder.

At least the colonel appeared calm, despite the handcuffs now circling his wrists, a nasty black eye, split lip, and a cut on his forehead.

"Where is she?" Burke demanded. His gaze darted from one corner of the room to the other. "Where is Libby?"

"She's safe. Tucked away in a place you'll never find her." Hands raised in front of him, Jude eased forward.

"Stop!" Burke swung the gun toward him, toward Pruitt, then back to him again. Unsure of who was the bigger threat. Good.

Jude slid another step closer. "You might as well put the gun down. I called the cops. They'll be here any minute."

"Then I have to make this fast." He pressed the gun to Pruitt's head again. "Take me to Libby."

"You're not going to get away." Another step. "We've seen you. We know who you are."

"So you'll have to kill each other. There's so much bad blood between the pair of you, nobody will doubt that. Especially not after I tell them what happened eight years ago. By the time the police are through, they'll uncover every bit of that nastiness. I'll tell them I tried to stop you, but Elliot attacked you because he was so enraged that you had your disgusting hands all over his daughter." His voice lifted to a near screech on the words. Yeah, it wasn't Pruitt who was pissed off about their relationship. Or at least not at the moment—the colonel would definitely have something to say about it later. Right now, Burke was the threat, and maybe he could use that anger to his advantage.

"If you know about that, then you know I couldn't care less if you killed the colonel right now." Out of the corner of his eye, he saw a flash of movement and prayed it was only the cat. "In fact, you'd be doing me a favor."

Pruitt's jaw tightened, and his eyes flashed, promising

hell to pay later. Jude ignored it.

"Libby will never go with you," he continued, hoping the lawyer would try something stupid in a fit of rage. "Not after you kill the two men she loves."

Burke vibrated with fury. "She loves *me*!"

Shit, that was no cat slinking around the edge of the room.

Cursing inwardly, Jude forced himself not to look at her and caught the colonel's gaze. If they were going to make a move, it had to be now. Pruitt nodded. He was ready.

They acted simultaneously, like a well-rehearsed dance. Pruitt looped his arms over Burke's head and pulled the chain of the handcuffs tight across his throat. Jude swept out with a leg and took his knees out with a kick. He sagged, but only for a second. Whatever malfunction in his head made him think that Libby loved him had apparently also immunized him to pain, and the lack of oxygen from the handcuff chain only whipped him into a frenzy.

Jude leaped forward to help contain the guy. An elbow jabbed his ribs. A sneaker glanced off his thigh and dug into the vulnerable spot between his legs. Fuck! Pain shoved his stomach into his throat, and he doubled over.

Burke lifted the gun and fired wildly. The bullet ricocheted off a ceiling fan and splintered the wood. The kickback sent his arm flailing and knocked the colonel off balance. Together they bounced off the back of the couch, crashed into the dining table. Chairs fell, the sturdy table skidded across the tile, and they both slammed into the floor with enough force to stun the breath out of anyone's lungs. Pruitt went limp for a moment, long enough that Burke squirmed his way out of the fight. He stood, limping, and gun still in hand, raised it to Jude's head.

Jude threw his weight forward and hit the floor flat on his stomach as the gun fired. Something glass shattered, raining water and shards over his head. A body thumped down beside him, and for one horrible moment, he thought, *Libby*.

But he opened his eyes and Burke lay next him, unconscious, a stream of blood flowing steadily from a cut in his temple. Libby stepped over Burke and kicked the gun away from his hand.

"Handcuffs," Pruitt groaned, still flat on his back several feet away. "Key's in his pocket. Get these off me and on him."

Libby knelt to go through the unconscious man's pockets and spared Jude a quick, worried glance. "Did he shoot you?"

Jude lifted himself to his hands and knees, shook away the cobwebs in his mind and ran through a mental checklist. He hurt, but in a general, not-moving-for-a-week kind of way, the pain originating from nowhere specific. Even the nausea from the ball busting was starting to fade.

"Nah. I'm good." He sat up on his knees and surveyed the scene as she unhooked the cuffs from her father's wrists and snapped them around Burke's like an old pro. Slivers of glass sparkled in puddles of water on the tile floor. "What the fuck did you hit him with?"

"A vase."

Pruitt stared at her in horror. "A what?"

Jude laughed, and pain spiked through his ribs. A vase. After all that, a fucking vase ended it. It was almost too funny—but then it wasn't, because something colorful lay limp under Burke's head, a splash of pink that didn't belong.

Holding his breath, he reached out and extracted a flower from under Burke's cheek.

Chapter Twenty-Four

"You kept it."

"What?" Libby stopped worrying over her father and followed Jude's gaze to the limp flower he held between his fingers. "Oh. So now you notice."

"You even put it in a vase," Jude said in amazement. He lifted his head and stared at her. "You *kept* it."

That expression. God, she wished she had a camera because the mix of surprise and excitement on his face was picture worthy.

"I couldn't throw it away," she admitted and let her heart go all soft and melty at his smile, which started as a slow upward tilt of his lips and blossomed into a grin as beautiful as the flower had once been.

"You couldn't throw it away," he said as if savoring each word, then gave a whoop. Ignoring the glass on the floor, he leaped to his feet, closed the distance between them, and scooped her up into his arms. The kiss was soft but persistent, and she wound her arms around his neck, held on to him with everything she had as outside, police sirens screamed to a stop in front of the house.

Over. It was finally over. Which was a good thing, she told herself. No more stalker, no more threats, no more hiding.

So why had a lump lodged hard and hot halfway up her throat? And why were her eyes stinging?

Across the room, her father cleared his throat, and Jude abruptly set her back on her feet. His entire body hardened under her hands, his muscles going steely, jaw tightening, suppressed hostility humming through every vein and tendon. She glanced back and forth between the two of them. What had Kenneth meant when he spoke of the bad blood?

She opened her mouth to ask, but her father took hold of her elbow and pulled her away from Jude. "It's time for us to go home."

Yes, she supposed it was, but she didn't want to. The realization hit her full force in that moment as she watched Jude all but steam with rage, his hands opening and closing into fists at his sides. That's why she wanted to cry. No more hiding equaled no more Jude, and she wasn't ready to say good-bye again. Not yet. Not when he was finally starting to show his true colors after all these years.

As gently as she could, she extracted herself from her father's grasp and turned to give him a kiss on the cheek. "Dad, you know I love you, and I will do most anything for you, but I'm not going home yet." She felt Jude's surprise at her back as keenly as she saw the ripple of shock over her father's face. To drive the point home, she backed up until Jude's arms encircle her. "I have ten days of vacation time left, and I'm entitled to take them."

"Here?" her father demanded.

"Maybe. I like it here. I like the company."

Jude didn't make a sound, but with her back pressed against his chest, she felt him exhale with something a lot like relief. Her father, on the other hand, looked like he was going to blow his top. His teeth clenched so hard she heard the grind of them from across the room.

"Sweet pea," he said in the same let's-be-reasonable tone he'd used on her when she was a teenager. "That's not a good decision."

"I'm an adult," she reminded him. "I think it's time I start making my own decisions, good or bad." Then she gentled her voice. "Go home to Mom. I'm sure she's worried sick about you. Tell her I'm fine and I'll be home in a couple weeks."

A long, stubborn moment passed.

"All right. We'll have a talk when you get home." With that, her father spun on his heel and marched out to meet the cops, barking orders at them as if they were his men.

"Holy shit," Jude muttered. "He actually listened to you."

"I didn't give him a choice." She turned in his arms to smile up at him. "Like I said, I'm an adult. It's past time he realizes that. I've indulged his need to hang on to his little girl long enough."

Jude's eyes rounded. "You've indulged him?"

"For years. Mostly, I just did what I wanted to do and then made him think it was his idea from the start. Like law school."

"You indulged him," he repeated slowly.

She smoothed her fingers over the frown lines that had

appeared in his forehead. "Yes, of course. Did you really think I'd let him dictate my every move? C'mon, Jude, you know me better than that."

"Well, shit."

"What?"

He shook his head. "I'm a fucking idiot."

"I've been trying to tell you that for weeks."

"No, I've been one for much longer. I—"

A phone rang. Libby had forgotten she'd slipped his cell into her shorts pocket before coming out to face Kenneth. She grabbed it, checked the screen, then held it up to him. "Your brothers."

"Yeah, I should take that." He removed the phone from her hand, but hesitated. "Uh, Libby…"

"Hm?"

His mouth worked as if he was struggling to find the words he wanted to say. Finally, he just shook his head again, turned away, and lifted the phone to his ear. "Hey, Cam."

She watched him walk away, frowning a little herself. What was that all about?

That afternoon, the skies opened up, and rain fell in sheets, splashing into the pool and sounding like bullets against on the tin roof of the portico. Thunder rumbled, long and low. Lightning flickered over the tops of the palms.

Libby curled up in the wicker love seat and basked in the warmth of the blaze Jude had started in a slate and marble fire bowl. The rain was so loud that she could barely hear the crackle of the flames, but she enjoyed the storm. It seemed like a fitting end to a day that had included multiple interviews with the police followed by another go-round with her father about her relationship with Jude. He'd said it was dangerous, reminded her of the wreck she'd been after Jude left last time.

But that was then. They were both different people now, and she could admit to herself that she wanted to see what would happen between them. Maybe it wouldn't last when they left Key West and returned to D.C., but she wouldn't know unless she took this chance. And she wouldn't be able to get on with her life until she knew for sure.

Jude appeared in the doorway, two mugs of coffee in hand. He left the French doors open, and music carrying the sounds of the tropics drifted out. "Did I miss anything?"

"Saw some lightning." She curled her legs up to her chest to make room for him.

"Bolt or flash?"

"Flash."

"Mm." He sat, handed her one of the mugs, and slung an arm along the back of the seat as he sipped from his own.

They watched the storm for a long time in silence, his fingers playing with a strand of her hair, her toes tucked underneath his thigh for warmth. The music, the rain, the fire… It was so perfect she didn't want to ruin it with more conversation, but it was time. She had questions for him, ones that had waited too many years for answers.

Sitting up, she set her empty mug on a side table and turned to face him. After a moment, he met her gaze. Gave one nod, finished off what was left of his coffee, and set his mug down beside hers.

"You know what I want to say," she started.

"Yeah, got an idea."

"Will you give me a direct answer?"

He hesitated. "You won't like it."

She exhaled as if she'd been holding her breath for nearly a decade. "It can't be any worse than wondering for eight years what I did wrong."

"Nothing." He looked stricken and angled his body so that they sat face-to-face. "Libs, you did nothing wrong, okay? It was all me. I thought I—" He stopped short.

"Thought you could have your cake and eat it, too?" she offered. "That's what Dad told me. He said all you young Marines were the same—it was just a part of your lifestyle. You didn't know how to commit. I didn't believe him, but he tried so hard to cheer me up afterward. Took me to ball games, even suffered through a Renaissance fair because he knew I liked them. He can be a jerk, but he has such a big heart, and it's always in the right place."

Jude's jaw tightened. "I know."

She waited, but he didn't seem inclined to say more.

"Jude, it's okay. I get it. We were so young, and we rushed everything."

His shoulders slumped, the steel going out of his spine. "Yeah. Yeah, that's it." There was an odd hollowness to his voice and a flatness in his eyes that she decided to analyze later because she was just too damn happy that he was *finally* talking to her.

"I was young," he said. "Had no impulse control."

Working up a smile, she poked him in the side. "And you do now?"

"I've learned. It's still not my greatest strength, but there are some lines that I won't cross. That's one of them."

"So where does that leave us?"

"I don't know. I guess that's up to you." He lifted his gaze, and his beautiful blue eyes were as serious as she'd ever seen them. "But I do know I want a second chance."

And here it was, she thought. The choice. Now that there was no reason to stay together, the smart thing to do would be to leave the past in the past, let these last few weeks go down as a pleasant fling, and go their separate ways. No damage. That's what the old Libby would do, but this experience had changed her. He had changed her, and the new Libby wasn't so adverse to a little risk. Some things were worth it.

Jude was worth it.

She closed the distance between them and laid her hands on his cheeks, pressing her lips to his. "I seem to have two weeks left of my vacation with nothing to do."

He caught her waist and dragged her onto his lap. "Is that so?"

"Unless you have some ideas."

"Tons." His lips skimmed the tendon along the side of her neck. "But I need to warn you, babe. Most involve a bed." Grinning, he scooped her into his arms and placed the cover over the fire bowl to douse the flames.

"Sounds like fun. But, Jude?" As he carried her toward the bedroom, she nipped his ear, flicked his earring with her tongue, and felt his groan rumble through his entire body. "Don't call me babe."

"You got it." His lips twitched. "Baby."

She sighed and settled her head on his chest. This was one battle she wasn't going to win. Time to plea bargain. "Okay, you can call me baby or babe—whatever—as long as I can call you Sugar Cheeks."

"Sugar Cheeks. I like it. Suits me."

She laughed. "You're hopeless."

"You wouldn't have me any other way." Jude kicked open the bedroom and playfully tossed her on the bed. She bounced once, but then he was there, his big body covering hers, his mouth claiming and devouring, until the storm outside paled in comparison to the one raging between them.

Chapter Twenty-Five

Jude downed the shot of Jack the bartender set in front of him and then went back to nursing his beer. The call he'd expected all day had come in just before midnight. He'd set his phone on vibrate so as not to wake Libby and snapped it up before the end of the first ring, intent on telling Colonel Pruitt to go fuck himself.

He never got the words out. They stuck in his throat, caught and held by all of his personal demons, just like they had eight years ago.

After he hung up, he'd suddenly found himself unable to breathe with pressure building to uncomfortable heights inside his chest. He'd needed air and had planned only to go for a short walk. Somehow, he'd ended up on Duval Street and then in this bar. He barely remembered sitting down, but by the pleasant buzz he had going, he guessed he'd been here long enough to have had a few.

His discussion earlier with Libby weighed heavily on

him. He should've told her the truth about what happened eight years ago. When she brought it up, he'd had every intention of telling her, but then she started going on about how big of a heart her father had and he just…couldn't.

And, now, coupled with that phone call…

That was the crux of the matter, wasn't it? He'd never be able to tell her the full truth without hurting her, without forcing her to choose between him and her father. Any way he saw it, he was bound to break her heart, and damn, he didn't want to put her through that again. He never should have asked for a second chance.

"Hi. Mind if I join you?"

Jude lifted his gaze from the depths of his beer, focused on the woman who had sidled up into his personal space and pressed her surgically enhanced breasts to his arm.

She didn't wait for his answer and sat on the empty stool next to his. Her skirt hiked up her thigh, leaving nothing to the imagination. "I'm Sienna."

"Hello, Sienna," he said politely, but had to wonder if that was even her real name. He lifted his glass and clinked it to the rim of her margarita. "Jude."

"Like the Beatles song?"

"Yeah," he said on a resigned sigh. Different bar, different woman, same old conversation. Usually, he played it up but not tonight. Tonight, he was tired of it all. It felt like they were rehearsing a scene off a well-used script. "Like the song."

"Sorry." She laughed. "I bet you hear that a lot."

He did a double take. Now this was an interesting diversion from that script. "All the time. I've even heard it used as a pick-up line."

"If you'd like, I'm sure I can think of something cute, but I'm not as subtle as that. I see a hot guy, I introduce myself, carry on some light conversation, then ask if he wants to go back to my place for the night. So…you interested?"

Jude turned on his stool to give her an assessing up-down. She was exactly the type he went for when he came to places like this. All glitter and gloss with an undercurrent of desperation. She wore a mini strapless dress tight enough to strangle, with her breasts nearly spilling out the top, and looked a mere shade better than a streetwalker only because she obviously had money and liked to spend in on bling—the real stuff, not gaudy imitations, if that huge diamond on her finger was any clue.

A wedding ring never used to be a deterrent to him. Now he found himself wondering why he'd ever thought that ring meant nothing but empty promises.

Cam was right. Their mother would be disgusted by him. Hell, he was disgusted by himself.

"I'll give you points for honesty, but no." One truth, he supposed, deserved another. He reached into his pocket and pulled out the ring he'd kept there for eight long years. The diamond was small, pathetic really, but all he'd been able to afford as a freshly minted second lieutenant. He'd bought it the morning after spontaneously popping the question during their celebratory dinner after his commissioning ceremony. He still wasn't entirely sure what made him ask Libby right then—he'd just looked over the table at her in her little black dress as the waiter cleared their plates, and realized he never wanted to be without her, so he'd let the question fly over dessert. Part of him had steeled up for the rejection he thought for sure was coming, but she'd said yes. Without a ring. Without even a real "I love you" from him. She'd said yes, and that still amazed him to this day.

Jude remembered the way the tiny diamond had sparkled when he'd given it to her—almost as bright as her smile. It had looked so lovely on Libby's finger, and he wanted nothing more than to see it there again.

He showed Sienna the ring. "I might've taken you up your offer at one time, but you're about a month too late."

"Oh," she said with a hint of disappointment. "Good for you. When's the big day?"

"Soon, I hope."

"You haven't asked her yet?"

"No."

Sienna laughed. "Well, what are you waiting for? You're obviously a one-woman man. Make it official already."

Damn, Jude thought as her words struck a chord inside him. He *wasn't* the least bit interested in any woman but Libby. His Libby, all soft and warm in their bed. He should be there with her now, arms tucked around her, his face buried in her hair, his leg trapping both of hers.

Libby was it for him. His all. His everything.

He'd always known he loved her, but kept pushing it away. Making excuses for himself because, fuck, what had he done to deserve a woman like her in his life? Maybe it was a big cosmic joke, but he didn't care anymore because he was never letting her go again.

"Thank you," he said and pocketed the ring.

Sienna's lips puckered into a frown. "For what?"

"For making me see what a fool I am." He finished his beer in one swallow, peeled off several bills from his wallet for the tip. "I'm going to tell her the truth. All of it. Maybe then I'll have a shot at making it forever. A real shot."

Sienna's hard blue eyes softened as she reached up, flicked a lock of hair off his forehead with a finger, then dragged one talon-like nail lightly down the side of his jaw. "She's a lucky woman."

"You wanna tell her that?"

"Oh, I'm sure she knows it. Deep in her heart, she knows."

S he should've known. As soon as she felt Jude leave the bed, as soon as he left the house and she decided to follow him, she should've known they'd end up here.

Libby stopped cold just inside the door of the bar as the past flashed before her eyes. Except it wasn't the past. It was happening again, right now, in living color. The brunette with the skin-tight dress showcasing a great body, tracing a nail along his jaw, her body language screaming come-and-get-me. Jude fresh from bed with Libby, his hair still mussed from her fingers, smiling, learning toward the woman...

No. Not again. She wasn't watching it happen again. Wasn't even going to confront him about it again. He didn't deserve even that much effort.

Bastard.

With angry tears burning her eyes, she slammed through the door and hailed one of the pink cabs sitting on the street. Yes, the hurt was there, and she was sure it'd come out later to torment her, but right now it was buried so deep under a layer of pissed off that it barely rated. God, she'd been such a fool thinking he'd changed. Players *always* play—and the stupid thing was she had known that from the start. So why was she surprised? This was her own damn fault for letting herself fall for him yet again.

Last Man on Earth Wilde.

"Stupid. Stupid, stupid, stupid." She kicked the seat in front of her with each word, and the driver eyed her in the rearview mirror.

"Hey, you gonna do that to my car, you can walk."

"Sorry." She pushed her hands through her hair and sucked in a calming breath. Realized she'd knocked her glasses askew and straightened them with as much dignity as she could muster. "I just caught the man I love cheating. Again."

The driver's expression softened. "Lotta that around here, unfortunately. People get drunk off booze and island life and lose their minds."

She straightened the hem of her lightweight jacket, which had bunched up around her belly during her tantrum. "That implies he had a mind to lose in the first place."

"Ah-ha. Good point. A man would have to be mindless to cheat on you."

Since the driver was at least as old as her grandfather, she took that as a compliment and not a come-on. "Thank you. You're very kind."

He shifted the car into gear. "Where do you want to go? I imagine away from here."

"Far away," she agreed. "The airport."

The driver left her to her thoughts after that, and she watched the party atmosphere of Duval give way to quiet, residential neighborhoods. She should tell the driver to change directions so she could go back to the house and pack. Maybe even leave a note for Jude because despite him cementing his spot as the King of Assholes tonight, he would worry if she just up and disappeared.

Libby scoffed at herself. What did she care? Let him worry. Served him right and, although she regretted not being able to say good-bye to Sam, she couldn't go back to Seth's house. She might break something—like Jude's thick scull if he decided to come home tonight after his dalliance with the brunette. She'd just have her father send someone for her things and catch the first available flight back to Miami. From there, it was only a two-and-a-half-hour flight home.

Oh God. Her father. Why hadn't she listened to him in the first place? She just hoped that he didn't resort to his father-knows-best speech, which was essentially a long I-told-you-so. She didn't think she could handle that now.

Libby leaned her head against the cab's seat and shut her eyes, blocking out the passing scenery, sick to death of palm trees and beaches and ocean.

This vacation was officially over.

The moment Jude stepped into the house and heard the particular echo that only came with emptiness, panic roared through him like a tsunami. Still, he checked every room, found the bed still rumpled from their earlier lovemaking, her clothes still in the dresser, toiletries still in the bathroom, her book still on the coffee table in the living room.

What if…?

No. He shut down the thought before it completely formed. Burke was in prison. With the stalking charges, Pruitt's abduction, and after his confession to K-Bar's murder, he was never getting free. The danger to her had passed.

Tell that to his heart, which was trying to pound out of his chest. He grabbed his cell phone from his jeans pocket and dialed Camden, who answered groggily after a handful of rings.

"What the hell, Jude? It's two o'clock. I just got to sleep."

"Libby's gone."

"Gone?" he repeated.

"Yes, gone, goddammit! She's not in the house! I can't find her!" Some distant portion of his fear-drenched mind realized he was screaming into the phone, but he didn't give a fuck.

"Whoa, relax." Cam sounded wide-awake now. "Take a breath."

He couldn't. For real this time, he couldn't breathe. He sank to the couch as his legs gave out and dropped his head forward between his knees. "She's gone. Did Burke…? Is he still…? Fuck." His voice broke. "What if she's in trouble?"

"She's not."

"You don't know that. We need to get the cops back out here. We need to make sure Burke's still locked up. She's gone!"

Silence stretched for eternity on his brother's end of the line. Finally, Cam sighed. "Are you drunk?"

"No, I'm not drunk!"

"Jude," Cam said evenly, "you need to calm the fuck down and listen to me, okay? Libby is not missing. She's on her way back to D.C."

"What?"

"Yeah, I thought you knew. Her father called Reece an hour ago and asked for travel arrangements for her from Miami. She should be in the air, on her way there now."

Jude opened his mouth, but his vocal chords seized. Why would she just up and leave like that?

And then he knew, the realization like a sucker punch to the gut. She'd followed him to the bar, had seen Sienna proposition him and…

Yeah. Given their past, that would make her bolt for sure.

So much for his second chance. Angry with himself, Jude hung up the phone and pulled the ring out of his pocket. He stared at it for a long, long time, turning it, watching the light play through the tiny gem. No sense in keeping it now, but… he folded his fingers around it and returned it to its home in his pocket so it could continue to torture him for the rest of his life.

He should have figured he'd fuck it all up. That's what he did best.

Chapter Twenty-Six

If one more person asked her if she was okay, she was going to scream.

Libby thought she couldn't wait to get back to work and dive into her normal life, and now she wanted nothing more than to go home and forget about all the whispers and pitying stares from well-meaning coworkers. Maybe curl up in her air-conditioned house with a book and a glass of ice tea. Even a week later, her body still hadn't acclimated back to D.C.'s changeable weather, and the windless summer day made the air soup-like. Her blouse stuck to her spine as she left her office building.

She double-timed it across the parking lot to her car. No doubt about it, the words "air conditioning," "book," and "ice tea" were synonyms for heaven, especially in this kind of weather. The only thing that could possibly make her night better would be a cat curled up on top of her feet.

The thought brought on a sharp stab of longing. She

missed Sam.

Maybe it was time to think about getting herself a cat. It would mean less time in the office, but maybe it was time for that, too. Maybe she needed to focus on something other than work.

She hit the button on her key fob to unlock her Subaru's doors, and as she reached for the handle on the driver's side, she sensed movement behind her. Not Kenneth, she told herself. Still, her heart tripped, her fingers slipped off the door handle, and she dropped her keys.

Not Kenneth. Not Kenneth. Not Kenneth.

But what if he'd gotten out…?

Working up a horror movie scream just in case, she whirled—and found her father.

She swallowed the scream with some effort and took the time to reach for her keys on the pavement at her feet before facing him. "What are you doing here?"

"I was driving by," he said in a light, casual tone. "I saw you coming out of the office and thought I'd stop."

He was so full of bullshit, and it ticked her off that he felt the need to gloss over his true intentions. "You're checking up on me."

"I'm your father."

"And I'm twenty-nine years old!" Libby wrenched open her car door, threw her briefcase inside, jammed the keys into the ignition, and started the engine. She'd been meaning to have this conversation with him but hadn't had the energy since returning home. Nevertheless, there were things that needed to be said, things that she couldn't put off any longer.

With the car A/C blasting, she straightened and turned back to him. "Dad, this has to stop."

"I don't know what you mean."

"Yes," she said more gently, "you do. I know everything you do is out of love, but it's too much. It's smothering. You have to stop."

"You're my daughter. It's my job to protect you."

"You can't protect me from everything. If you try, it's going to drive a wedge between us." And as much as he sometimes annoyed her, the thought of losing him over something so fixable, of never seeing him again due to their shared stubborn gene, made her throat tighten up. "I don't want that. I want you in my life, Daddy—just not controlling it."

His shoulders hunched slightly, which she hadn't thought possible. He always walked, stood, ate, and probably even slept with the erect posture of a Marine in formation. In her entire life, she'd never seen him slouch. "I just want you safe and happy."

She rubbed his arm. "I am safe now." Happy was another beast altogether, one she hadn't tamed yet. True, for a short time in Key West, she'd thought…

But that was over.

She'd make her own happiness, starting tomorrow. She'd go to the animal shelter and pick out a cat. She'd cut back her hours at work, find a hobby or two, and eventually start dating again. In time, she'd find her own kind of happiness.

She supposed she had Jude to thank for that. She'd been frozen in the past for eight long years, unable to move forward, but three weeks in paradise with him had started thawing her. Then his betrayal had cracked away the last of the ice, leaving her exposed, forcing her to make a decision. Change or perish.

She chose change.

Her father was staring at her with worry pinching his eyes, the creases radiating outward until they disappeared under the edge of his service uniform cover. "You're not happy."

"No," she admitted. "But I will be."

The air settled thickly in the silence that fell between them.

Finally, in another uncharacteristic move, he shifted on his feet. "What happened between you and Wilde after I left Key West?"

"Dad…" She sighed. Okay, so change wouldn't be easy, especially not for someone like her father. She had a feeling this was the first of many similar conversations. "I thought we just discussed this. What happened is none of your business."

"No, I think it is." He motioned to her car. "Get in."

"Why?"

"I have a story to tell you."

She stared at him for a moment. She wanted to stand her ground and demand he explain himself, but the coolness inside her car beckoned. She slid behind the wheel, waited until he walked around the hood and slid into the passenger seat. Then she turned to him, suspicion making her voice sharper than she'd planned. "What kind of story exactly?"

Sighing, he pulled off his cover and rubbed a hand over his hairless head. Libby had always liked his baldness. He used to bend over as he tucked her in every night so she could kiss the crown of his head. The memory made her smile inwardly. If there was one constant in her life, it was her father's love.

"It's the story," he began without meeting her gaze, "of a father trying to protect his daughter. Of him taking it a step too far when she fell in love with a man he didn't want her with."

Libby sucked in a breath. "Oh my God, Dad. What did you do to Jude? Is he okay?"

He flinched as if her words had slapped him across the face. "He's fine. Back home, working with his brothers. I wouldn't hurt him, and it shames me that you think I would."

"I don't! At least—I just—The way you said—" She pressed her lips together and took a second to gather her wits. "What did you mean by that?"

"I was talking about the past."

Her stomach sank into her toes. "When?"

"Jude came to our house one day eight years ago in full uniform, even saluted when he saw me. He'd come to ask me for my blessing to marry you."

She could picture it so clearly, Jude walking into the lion's den in full dress uniform. Saluting her father. Asking his question...and getting shot down. "You told him he didn't have your blessing, didn't you?"

Misery radiated off him as he shook his head. "I didn't want you marrying a Marine."

"How could you?"

He finally met her gaze, and in his eyes, she saw his shame, but also a kind of desperation she'd never seen before. "Elizabeth, do you have any idea what I put your mother through every time I left for a tour? Neither of us wanted that for you. I didn't want to take the risk you'd end up a young, heartbroken widow. Or, God forbid, a young widow with young children to care for. I wanted you to finish school, make a career for yourself."

Tears blurred her vision, and she blinked them furiously back. "Who says I wouldn't have?"

"Statistics."

She shook her head in disbelief. "What about what I wanted?"

"It wasn't a consideration," he admitted. "It's my job to protect you."

Funny, Jude once said those exact same words to her.

"Dad…" But she couldn't yell at him. He was obviously already aware of his mistake so what would yelling accomplish? "Oh, Daddy."

"A day later, I found out he'd already proposed to you before he ever came to ask my permission." He hung his head. "It was not one of my proudest moments. I had this ugly idea of your future embedded in my mind, and I thought I had to stop it, so I tracked Jude down, roughed him up a little, threatened to ruin his career, his life, to poison you against him while he was overseas. That last bit broke him. You should know he would have endured all of the rest, would have put up with me making him miserable for the rest of his life, but the thought of returning home to find out you hated him—that broke him."

You've indulged him?

The surprise in Jude's voice at that realization suddenly made a lot more sense. For years, he'd thought her father had absolute sway over her. What must have gone through his head when he found out that wasn't the case?

I'm a fucking idiot.

Oh, he wasn't the only one in this situation. She punched her father's shoulder as hard as she could. His head snapped up in surprise, and his eyes flashed anger followed by hurt.

"*That* was for ruining the best thing I ever had!" It wasn't until he reached over and folded her in his arms that she realized she was crying freely. He rocked her as he had in her childhood when soothing her from a nightmare.

"I'm so sorry, Libby. As much as I try—" His voice broke. "I'm not perfect. I hope someday you can forgive me."

She held on to him as tightly as she could and buried her tears in the front of his uniform. "He cheated on me again. After you left, I followed him to a bar and saw him with another brunette. Why is it always a brunette?"

"Oh, sweetie, no." Firmly, he set her away from him and wiped at her tears with his big thumbs. "I don't know what you think you saw, but it wasn't Jude Wilde cheating. For all of his faults, he's not a cheater. He never has been."

She sniffled. "He cheated before."

"No. I told him he had to break things off with you in a way that you'd never want to take him back. The woman you saw him with? She was another Marine. I asked her to help him with the charade."

"You *made* him hurt me?"

Her father nodded. "I thought it was for your own good, but I was wrong. He's not a cheater."

"Then what was he doing with that brunette on Duval Street?"

He drew a breath. "I called him that night and warned him away from you again."

"Dad!"

"It was wrong, I know, but maybe that's why he was at the bar. You should go ask him." He pressed a kiss to her forehead, then let her go and placed his cover back on his head. As he pushed open the car door, he hesitated and looked at her for a long moment. "And tell him…he has my blessing."

Chapter Twenty-Seven

Jude snarled as a shadow fell over the papers on his desk, blocking out the crappy office lights. He'd spent his week up to his elbows in the expense reports Reece demanded he fill out, and he just wanted to finish this last one, go home, and drown his sorrows for the weekend.

He didn't want to talk to anyone and thought the F-U force field he'd constructed around himself would keep them all at bay. Then again, some of his brothers had no concept of self-preservation.

He lifted his gaze and scowled at the owner of the shadow. Camden stood beside the desk unapologetically blocking the light with his big frame. Sam the Cat lay across Cam's wide shoulders, content to hang there like a fluffy orange scarf and doze. Since Jude had no idea when Seth would be home, he'd brought the feline back to D.C. with him, and Sam had quickly won over the hearts of his brothers, earning himself a spot as Wilde Security's spoiled mascot.

"You're in my light," Jude snapped.

"Yup."

"I'm busy. What do you want?"

"For starters," Cam said, "my brother back."

"What are you talking about? I'm right here."

"Where are the paper footballs? The fight provoking? You haven't even aggravated Reece once since you got home."

"I'm okay with that," Reece said from across the room.

"Yeah, well, I'm not." Camden took the cat off his shoulders, plopping the fat feline down on top of Jude's reports. "How about a game of Battleship?"

Libby, accusing him of cheating as she tossed her panties at him…

As his gut twisted, he shut his eyes to close out the memory. "I hate that game."

"Since when?"

He shooed Sam off his desk, picked up his pen, and got back to work, but Cam yanked the paper out from under the tip.

"Okay, this has got to stop. Go find her."

"No."

"Why the hell not?" Cam demanded.

"Because I don't want to."

"Bullshit," Cam said. "Try again."

"Because I don't fucking care."

Cam made a buzzer sound out of the side of his mouth. "You're oh-for-two. One more time."

Jude glared up at his brother. "She doesn't want me, okay? Now leave me the fuck alone."

"Ah, getting warmer."

"Goddammit!" All of the hurt and sorrow coalesced into

a blinding rage so hot he didn't realize he whipped his pen at the desk hard enough to break the cheap thing until Sam jumped and hissed. Except for scaring the cat out of one of his nine lives, the splintered pen bounced harmlessly to the floor. Wasn't enough. Anger rode him so hard he wanted to throw the whole damn desk across the room. It didn't help that all of his brothers had stopped what they were doing to eavesdrop, and Cam stood there, arms crossed, looking so calm and reasonable and Cam-like, prompting him to spill his guts with a murmured, "Talk to me, bro."

Jude opened his mouth, but the fuck off he'd formulated in his mind came out as a broken whisper instead. "I don't deserve her."

The whole room went utterly still, and all of his brothers stared at him as if he'd just announced he wanted a sex change.

"What?" Camden breathed.

"I don't deserve her," he repeated, enunciating each word. "I don't deserve to be happy."

"What makes you think that?" Greer stepped out of his office doorway, where he'd paused to listen in on the convo. He crossed the room and stopped in front of Jude's desk.

"Because... Shit. Just because." Leaning back in his chair, he stared his brothers. Greer—strong, silent, intense, and hiding more secrets than any of them. And, damn, the guy looked so much like Dad, Jude couldn't bear it. Not now. Not when every wound he'd ever hidden behind a smile was raw and open and throbbing.

He turned his gaze to Reece—all focus and practicality, a lot like Libby. At one time, a very long time ago, he'd been closer to Reece than any of them. Now a lifetime of slights had built up to the point that they could barely stand to be in the same room together, and he suspected a lot of that was his fault.

The twins. Cam—easygoing and so rock steady a hurricane wouldn't budge him. Vaughn—direct and decisive, a little rough around the edges, a fighter. He'd gotten them both into trouble more times than he could remember.

And then there was him. Jude, the fuck up.

"I hate myself," he told them, all heat gone from his voice. After the confession left his lips, he thought he should feel lighter. Relieved or some shit that it was all out in the open now. He didn't. He wasn't. Exhaustion dragged him down, but he kept talking anyway. "I've always hated myself, but I have to grin and bear it because that's my punishment."

Greer planted his hands on the desktop and leaned in. "I think you need to open that big yap of yours and start talking. Really talking. No more bullshit. What do you mean, *punishment*?" Despite his harsh tone, worry shone in his eyes, which only made Jude's throat tighten up more.

"You look like Dad."

Greer straightened like he'd been poked in the ass with a Bowie knife. "What did you say?"

"I see it more every day. Sometimes it hurts to look at you and know…"

Greer's mouth worked soundlessly as he struggled to find something to say. Cam nudged him aside and sat on the edge of the desk. "Hey, man, we all miss them."

Jude nodded. True enough. His brothers had all had a little more time to make good memories with their parents. On the other hand, he'd been so young, not even a teenager yet. Out of the few memories he could recall, the worst was the one that stood out the most, a streak of blood red across what would otherwise have been a flawless childhood. "But none of you killed them."

"What the fuck?" Vaughn said. "You were just a kid. You didn't kill them."

"Yeah, I did." Jude looked over at Reece, expecting confirmation, and instead seeing a face not quite like Dad's that had gone ghost white. The memory of that night played out in his older brother's expression: thirteen-year-old Reece pulling him out of bed, cursing at him, trying to figure out how to alert their parents that the crisis had passed. The police knocking on the door hours later. Child services coming to take them all away to different homes and Reece turning on him with hatred in his eyes...

It's all your fault. They're dead because of you!

Greer frowned at the two of them. "Jude, listen to me. What happened to Mom and Dad wasn't your fault, and whatever happened between the two of you"—he wagged a finger in the air between him and Reece—"you need to take care of it. Now. It's long overdue." He turned, motioned a c'mon gesture to Cam and Vaughn. "Twins, let's give them some space."

The door shut behind them, and silence descended like a torrential rain, cold and heavy. Reece still hadn't moved. Hadn't even blinked. His body was present, but his mind wasn't. Jude suspected he was still twenty years away, reliving the worst night of their lives, and stayed silent. He didn't expect much to come from this little heart-to-heart—the pain ran too deep, the wound had festered too long. He couldn't see how a simple conversation would change that.

Reece finally stirred. He shut his eyes and released a shaky breath. When he finally lifted his lids, moisture spiked his lashes.

"All this time, you thought…?" His voice came out thick, raw. With a shaking hand, he loosened his tie and fumbled with the buttons of his collar, but gave up after his hand proved too unsteady. He paced away, circled the twins' desks, and came back. "Fuck. I didn't mean anything I said that day."

"I know."

"No, I don't think you do."

"Let's just forget it."

"Jude, I was angry, grieving—" He swallowed hard and dragged his hands over his short, dark hair. "But so were you and that's not an excuse. I should have protected you, taken care of you. You were only a child. Instead, I accused you. I should have realized you'd take it to heart. I…ruined you."

A lump the size of an aircraft carrier lodged in Jude's throat, but he forced a smile. "I wouldn't say *ruined*."

"You're so full of shit. You think you don't deserve a woman like Libby Pruitt when you're obviously head over heels for her. You think you don't deserve to be happy—all because of something I said out of grief twenty years ago. How is that not ruined?"

He didn't have an answer to that and just shook his head. Denial was his good friend, and he slipped into its embrace easily. "Let's pretend this conversation never happened."

"Fuck that. You *do* deserve happiness. Mom and Dad would want you to be happy. *I* want you to be happy, and if this Libby woman does it for you, then I say go for it."

Christ, he wanted to, but even if Reece was right, even if he did deserve happiness—which he still doubted—there were too many other obstacles in the way. Namely, Colonel

Elliot Pruitt. "Her father warned me away from her. Again."

"So?"

Jude smiled, but this time it came easily. "Careful. You're starting to sound like me."

"Devil must be building an igloo."

"Must be." Maybe he wasn't ready to stop blaming himself for his parents' deaths yet, but damn, it felt good to know that Reece had never blamed him. And maybe, just maybe, his brothers had a point about Libby. He stood. "You know this doesn't mean I'm going to stop annoying you every chance I get."

"This doesn't mean I'm going to stop being annoyed," Reece said.

Jude didn't know who moved first, but in the next instant, they stood together in a tight, backslapping embrace.

Reece pulled away and clasped Jude's face in his hands, gave him an affectionate slap on the cheek like their father used to do. "Now go get your lady, bro."

Jude hit the parking lot at a run, car keys in hand. For once, he didn't mind that he was following an order given by Reece. He felt lighter somehow and damn if he wasn't going to do everything in his power to get Libby back. He could admit now that he missed her. That he still—

And there she was. Hurrying across the parking lot of the mostly abandoned strip mall where Greer had set up the Wilde Security office, her eyes shielded against the glare of the setting evening sun by her hand.

He skidded to a halt in surprise. "Libby."

She stopped walking a good ten feet from him. She wasn't wearing her glasses, but he remembered she once told him they fogged up in muggy weather like this so she only wore them indoors. Knowing such a little, unimportant detail about her thrilled him. He wanted more. He wanted everything.

Libby bit down on her lower lip, fiddled with the top button of her silky blouse. "Hi."

"Hi," he said back. Okay, lame response but his brain wasn't firing on all cylinders. "What are you doing here?" And, yeah, that wasn't any better. He winced and hoped she didn't take offense to that question.

She took several steps closer, but stopped still too far out of his reach. "I know why you cheated on me eight years ago."

"Yeah, well, I told you why back in Key West."

She shook her head. "I know the real reason. Dad threatened you."

Jude's heart started to pound a painful drumbeat against his ribs. Stupid reaction. Just because she now knew the truth didn't mean squat as far as their relationship went. "He told you?"

"He did," she confirmed and took another step closer. "He also told me about that woman, how she was a fellow Marine. You're not a cheater. Never have been."

Jude shut his eyes and savored those words, ones he never thought she'd say or even know. When he opened his eyes again, she stood directly in front of him, less than an arm length away.

"Let me hear you say it, Jude."

He moistened his lips. "Say what?"

"You know." She stepped into him and pressed her cheek to his chest. "Dad was only trying to protect me in his own way, but he robbed us of eight years together. Please don't make me wait a second longer."

His arms wrapped around her, pulling her tight against his body. "I love you, Libby."

She sniffled, and when she raised her head, tears streamed from her eyes. "I love you, too. I never stopped."

"Neither did I." Intent on doing it right this time, he dropped to one knee right there in the parking lot and dipped his hand in his pocket for the ring he'd carried for too many years. He held it out to her, his nerves rattling until he saw her sharp intake of breath as she recognized it. Then everything in him settled into a sense of rightness.

"Libby, will you honeymoon in Key West with me?"

She sank to her knees in front of him and stared at the ring with wonder. "You kept it."

"I've never been without it."

The tiny diamond sparked in the evening sun. She reached out, but hesitated as if touching it would destroy the perfection of the moment. He wanted to tell her nothing could, but instead grasped her hand and slid the ring into its rightful spot on her finger.

"I love you," he told her because he had eight years to make up for and only a lifetime in which to do it—not nearly enough time. "I want to marry you. Most of my adult life, all I've wanted was to marry you, start a family with you, live in domestic bliss with you until we're both old and crazy."

"You're already crazy."

"Depends on your definition." He grinned, and for the first time in a long time, his smile didn't hide any secret pain. "Is that a yes?"

Libby leaned forward and wound her arms around his neck. "It's definitely a yes."

Acknowledgments

Thanks to my fellow SHUer, Cody Langille, for sharing his experiences in Key West.

Thanks to my awesome editor, Heather Howland, for keeping me sane through this whirlwind.

And, Sue Winegardner, what would have I done without you on this one? Thanks for keeping me honest. You're an amazing fount of military-related information.

Finally, my family. Thanks for being patient with me.

About the Author

Writing has always been Tonya's one true love. She wrote her first novel-length story in 8th grade and hasn't put down her pen since. She received a B.A. in creative writing from SUNY Oswego and is now working on an MFA in popular fiction at Seton Hill University.

Tonya shares her life with two dogs and a ginormous cat. They live in a small town in Pennsylvania, but she suffers from a bad case of wanderlust and usually ends up moving someplace new every few years. Luckily, her animals are all excellent travel buddies.

When Tonya is not writing, she spends her time reading, painting, exploring new places, and enjoying time with her family.

www.tonyaburrows.com